**S**crew this, I thought. What was I doing there? Why in the world had I thought that being a camp counselor was a good way to spend my summer? R&R? *Ha!* I saw now that being a camp counselor was just another form of baby-sitting, but without the fresh DVDs and well-stocked refrigerator.

I didn't need this. I could walk away right then and there. I could say I wasn't feeling well, that I was homesick, that I wasn't comfortable working with burn survivors. True, I'd signed a contract with Mr. Whittle saying I'd work the whole summer, but it wasn't legally binding (the one good thing about being sixteen years old!).

I turned to look out the open door, to a world of freedom without shrieking kids.

And at that exact moment, Web walked by outside.

**Also by Brent Hartinger:**

*Geography Club*
*The Last Chance Texaco*
*Grand and Humble*

# THE ORDER OF THE
# POISON OAK

## BRENT HARTINGER

HarperTempest
*An Imprint of* HarperCollins*Publishers*

HarperTempest is an imprint
of HarperCollins Publishers.

The Order of the Poison Oak
Copyright © 2005 by Brent Hartinger
All rights reserved. Printed in the United States of America. No part of
this book may be used or reproduced in any manner whatsoever without
written permission except in the case of brief quotations embodied in
critical articles and reviews. For information address HarperCollins
Children's Books, a division of HarperCollins Publishers, 1350 Avenue
of the Americas, New York, NY 10019.
www.harperteen.com

Library of Congress Cataloging-in-Publication Data
Hartinger, Brent.
   The Order of the Poison Oak / by Brent Hartinger.—1st ed.
     p.   cm.
   Summary: After "coming out" at school, sixteen-year-old Russel
decides to take a counselor job at a camp for burn victims to get away
from the antagonism of his classmates, but finds that ten-year-old boys
have just as many problems as he does.
   ISBN-10: 0-06-056732-5 — ISBN-13: 978-0-06-056732-6
   [1. Camp counselors—Fiction. 2. Camps—Fiction. 3. Burns and
scalds—Fiction. 4. Homosexuality—Fiction.] I. Title.
PZ7.H2635Or 2005                                    2004006493
[Fic]—dc22                                                CIP
                                                          AC

Typography by Ali Smith
❖
First HarperTempest paperback edition, 2006

**For Laura South-Oryshchyn,**

*a founding member of the Order of the Poison Oak*

**And for Michael Jensen,**

*to whom I hereby grant a Lifetime Membership*

# Chapter One

I was surrounded by fires, angry blazes raging all around me. The flames hissed and crackled, their blistering heat searing my exposed skin. I desperately wanted to run, but there was no escape. I was trapped by the heat. Any step I might take, any direction I might turn, the flames would flare up and engulf me.

Then the school bell rang, and the students around me began bustling off to class.

I was standing in the hallway of Robert L. Goodkind High School in the moments before my first class. I was surrounded by flames, yeah, but not the kind you might think. No, the fires that threatened me were the flames of hatred and suspicion that flickered in the eyes of my classmates.

Why did I feel like the hallway of my high school was some perilous corridor of fire, and the looks in the eyes of the other students were the flames of that blazing inferno? There is a very short answer to that question: earlier in the year, some friends and I had started the Goodkind High Gay-Straight-Bisexual Alliance. And now the whole school knew I was gay.

Okay, so maybe I'm being melodramatic about the school being on fire. All I know is that ever since I'd come out, my high school had suddenly felt like a very dangerous place—and I had the defaced locker and anonymous E-mails to prove it.

"Move it, faggot," Nate Klane said as he ambled by me in the hallway.

See? This was exactly the kind of thing I'm talking about. I'd put up with this kind of crap ever since we'd gone public with our Gay-Straight-Bisexual Alliance, and frankly I was getting pretty tired of it. Yeah, yeah, sticks and stones can break my bones, but words can never hurt me. First of all, anyone who thinks that words can't hurt you has obviously never taken sophomore P.E. And second, did it ever occur to whoever wrote that stupid adage that hurtful words might be a pretty good indication that sticks and stones are on the way? It's not like it's an either-or thing. I mean, has there *ever* been a case of sticks and stones that didn't also involve at least some words? All I can say is that the writer of that adage sounds pretty damn blasé about getting his bones broken.

Let's face it: being openly gay at age sixteen really, really sucks. (And if you're saying, Well, then, why did you come out? it's not like being gay and closeted at age sixteen is some carnival in the cafeteria.) But since this is the first chapter of this book, I can't be all negative and overwrought or you won't want to read any more (I'm not pointing fingers—I hate books like that too). So I'll say the only positive thing I was thinking at the time.

Summer vacation was only four weeks away.

That morning, in a break between classes, I met my friend Gunnar by his locker. He was sniffing the air.

"Hey," I said.

"Do you smell something?" he said.

I took a whiff. "Jerry Mason's gym socks."

"Not that."

"What do you think you smell?" I asked him.

*"Aspergillus flavus."*

I was afraid to ask what that was.

"It's a toxic mold," Gunnar said. "I think

3

maybe our school has it."

Let me cut to the chase: my friend Gunnar was, in a word, weird. The fact that he was a hypochondriac was the least of his quirks. But he was also smart and creative and just an all-around great guy. Example: he wasn't gay, but he'd joined the Goodkind Gay-Straight-Bisexual Alliance out of loyalty to me.

"You ever hear of the curse of King Tut's tomb?" Gunnar said. I shook my head no. "Well, in the years after they opened that tomb, almost everyone on the expedition died. People said it was the Mummy's Curse. But now some people think that maybe the reason they died was because they were exposed to *Aspergillus flavus* when they opened the tomb."

As much as I liked Gunnar, I wasn't interested in toxic mold—even if the Egyptian mummy connection was kind of cool. So I decided to change the subject.

"Looking forward to summer?" I said.

"You know it," Gunnar said. There was a weary rumble in his voice that surprised me, even though it shouldn't have. Since Gunnar had joined the Goodkind Gay-Straight-Bisexual Alliance, he'd been on the receiving end of all the same crap as me. Only in his case, it was actually even worse. More than anything in the world, Gunnar wanted a girlfriend. He'd been trying to get one for years, but it had never worked out. (Being weird is not a plus when you're looking for a girlfriend, and being smart and creative aren't all that helpful either.) But now, thanks to the Goodkind Gay-Straight-Bisexual Alliance, everyone also thought he was gay. We'd tried to tell people that he wasn't gay—"It's the Gay-*Straight*-Bisexual Alliance, remember?"—but no one believed us. So now the one thing he most desperately wanted—a girlfriend—was the one thing he could never have. Not as long as he was a student at Goodkind High School, anyway.

"Hey," I said, "there's a stream cleanup the first weekend in June. You want to sign up?" The summer before, we'd volunteered for a stream cleanup and had met a couple of girls we'd talked to all afternoon. I'd had no interest in them, of course, and it hadn't led anywhere, even for Gunnar. But there'd probably be new girls this year. I figured helping Gunnar find a girlfriend was the least I could do for him, given that he'd joined the Gay-Straight-Bisexual Alliance for me.

To my surprise, Gunnar shook his head and said, "Nah."

He had obviously forgotten what had happened at the stream cleanup. "Remember last year?" I said. "We met those girls?"

He nodded. "I remember."

"They didn't go to our school. And there'll probably be other girls who don't go to our school." In other words, they wouldn't think Gunnar was gay.

"It's not that," he said. "I'm just not interested."

"In stream cleanups?"

"In girls."

This took a moment to compute. Gunnar not interested in girls? It made no sense. It was like talking about a diabetic honeybee.

"Gunnar," I said. "What is it?"

He slumped back against his locker. "I'm tired of it, Russ." My name is Russel Middlebrook, but Gunnar always calls me Russ. "Every time I get excited about some girl," he went on, "I just end up saying or doing the wrong thing. I'm tired of embarrassing myself, and I'm tired of the rejection."

I don't mean to be mean, but Gunnar wasn't exaggerating. Somehow he always did seem to end up embarrassing himself around girls. And that was even before the Gay-Straight-Bisexual Alliance.

"So what are you saying?" I asked.

"I'm saying I'm giving up girls," he said.

I stared at him like he'd just said he was giving up pants. Or oxygen. (Have I made myself clear on the strangeness of the whole Gunnar-giving-up-girls thing?)

"It's not forever," he said. "I just decided that maybe I'm trying too hard. So I'm going to give it a rest."

I nodded, trying to be supportive. In a way, it actually made sense. Then again, since when did people start doing the logical thing?

"Besides," Gunnar said, "I think I got a summer job."

"No kidding," I said. "Where?"

"Camp Serenity. It's this summer camp up in the mountains. I'm going to be a camp counselor."

I glared at him. "And you were going to tell me this *when*, exactly?" We were best friends. It wasn't like one of us to run off and leave the other alone all summer long.

"Give me a break," Gunnar said. "I just found out about it last night. And I still have to apply, but the camp director is a friend of my dad's. He says they're desperate."

As Gunnar was talking, I thought to myself, Up

7

in the mountains? As in, away from everyone and anyone who knew I was gay?

"What about me?" I said. "You think they'd take me too?"

Gunnar grinned. "That's what I was hoping you'd say!"

I was dying to tell my other best friend, Min, about our summer plans. She and Gunnar and I were all friends, and the only thing better than Gunnar and me going off to the mountains for the summer was the idea of Min coming with us. Min was a member of the Goodkind Gay-Straight-Bisexual Alliance too, only she had more of a reason to join than just loyalty to me. She was bi. She was also Chinese-American, which has nothing to do with anything, and which almost seems kind of racist to even bring up at this point. But her name sort of bears explanation.

I caught up with her in the hallway on the way to lunch. But before I could say a word, she nodded toward a guy in front of us and said, "Tim Noll is so hot! I love the way the hair on the back of his neck is so neatly trimmed."

"Min!" I said. More than anything, I just wanted her to keep her voice down.

"Oh, come *on*," Min said. "Don't tell me you haven't noticed him."

I *hadn't* noticed him. Ever since I'd come out as gay, I'd made it a point not to notice guys at all. When the whole school knows you're gay, the last thing you want is someone catching you looking at another guy. I couldn't think of any better way to bring on the sticks and stones I mentioned earlier.

"Min," I said, changing the subject, "Gunnar has this idea about what the three of us can do this summer."

She ignored me. "Or Jason Gelrecht. You know he got his teeth laser-whitened? Not that I spend a lot of time looking at his *teeth*." Ever since I'd come out as gay and Min had come out as bi, she seemed to like talking about hot guys with her gay best friend, especially when we were in public. But I don't think it was because she really cared about hot guys. No, I think it was more so she could prove that she didn't care what anyone thought of her. But it always made me uncomfortable, which I think was also partly the point. Min was one of my two best friends, but she could be kind of competitive. On some level, all her talk about hot guys was kind of a challenge to me: could I be as bold as her? (I know this makes her sound like a bit of a bitch. But she was always interesting to be around, and often pushed me to do things I wouldn't otherwise do.)

"Min," I said. "I'm serious. This friend of Gunnar's dad runs this summer camp, and he—"

"Or Jarred Gasner," Min said, "even though that's kind of a cliché, him being Homecoming King and all. I bet you've seen him in the shower, haven't you? What does he look like naked?"

Min and I may have been talking, but we definitely weren't communicating. So it was time to fight fire with fire.

"You know who I think is hot?" I said.

"Who?" Min said. I'd gotten her attention, at least.

"Jennifer Nance." Min was bi, but she never talked about which *girls* she thought were hot, which I thought was very interesting.

Min laughed. "Oh, touché! I wondered when you'd get around to trying that." One thing I appreciated about Min: she was smart—even smarter than Gunnar. She caught on to things fast, which always kept me on my toes. "Hey," she said, "we can talk about hot girls if you want! I think Amy Mandrake has a great tush."

Okay, I thought, Min had won another round, even if she had used an incredibly geeky word like "tush." But she had an advantage. She was a girl, and girls didn't have to worry nearly as much about sticks and stones and broken bones.

"Just listen to me a second," I said. "Gunnar is going to apply to be a counselor at a summer camp, and he—"

"I'm in," Min said.

"What?" I said.

"I want to go with you guys. I want to be a camp counselor too."

I knew Min was quick, but I'd never known her to be *this* quick before!

Min saw the startled expression on my face and laughed again. "Sorry. Gunnar told me all about it during biology lab."

In spite of her teasing me, I was pretty happy. I was going to be spending the summer in a place called Camp Serenity with my two best friends. I was certain it was going to be two months of the peaceful, completely non-gay R&R that I so desperately needed.

Looking back, I don't think I've been so wrong about anything in my whole entire life.

## Chapter Two

**So** the three of us got summer jobs as camp counselors. And four and a half weeks later, the Monday
morning after school let out, we all climbed into
Gunnar's car and drove up into the mountains.
Camp Serenity was located at the end of a dusty
gravel road on the shore of a long, narrow body of
water called—surprise!—Lake Serenity. The lake
itself was not quite as pretty as a postcard, but it
was much prettier than a snapshot. As for the
camp, it consisted of a grassy marching field with a
flagpole and a totem pole; a beach with a swimming area, huge fire pit, and dock; a lodge and
cafeteria on the hill above the beach; and ten cabins scattered in the trees along the water.

The first camp session didn't start until the

following Sunday, but we counselors had had to come a week early so the camp director could tell us what our jobs were all about. Min, Gunnar, and I had been hired for five two-week sessions. In other words, Camp Serenity was going to be my home for almost the whole summer. But I didn't mind. On the contrary, I was thrilled. I was with Min and Gunnar—the two people I cared more about than anyone in the world. And absolutely no one else within fifty miles knew I was gay. And they never *would* know, not if I could help it.

Gunnar parked the car in the gravel parking lot, and I suppose here is where I should tell more about how the camp looked, or how we went inside the lodge to talk to the camp director. Then again, that's all pretty boring, so I figure I can skip all that and get right to the interesting part.

His name was Web Bastian, and he was much prettier than any postcard.

Web—short for Webster, I guess—was one of the ten counselors who had been hired by the camp director, a pasty-faced bald man named Mr. Whittle. I know I said before that ever since I'd come out, I didn't notice hot guys, but (a) I meant at school, where everyone knew I was gay, and (b) that was a lie. When it came to Web, I could hardly keep my eyes off him.

"So!" Mr. Whittle said when we counselors had all gathered in a circle on the floor of the lodge's big common room. "Why don't we get started, okay? First, let me welcome you to Camp Serenity."

Mr. Whittle went on to introduce the four other adults who helped run the camp, but I barely heard a word he was saying. I was looking at Web while trying to pretend I *wasn't* looking (you know exactly what I mean). He was older than me—probably eighteen or nineteen—with dark hair and a face like the impossibly cute lead singer of some trendy-but-not-too-edgy garage band. And he had one of those lean, perfectly proportioned bodies where his clothes just sort of fell off him, like rain dripping from a weeping willow.

"Now," Mr. Whittle was saying, "I see a couple of familiar faces from years past, which I guess means we're doing something right, huh? Why don't we go around in a circle and everyone can introduce themselves, okay?"

Web was the seventh person to introduce himself, and that's when I heard his voice for the first time. "I'm Web Bastian," he said, and his voice was deep like an ocean, but gentle like a lake. And speaking of lakes and oceans, I didn't mention Web's eyes, which were bluer than a tropical lagoon.

I was still thinking about Web when I heard Mr. Whittle say, "Now, I need everyone to divide up into pairs. And let's all pair up with someone we don't know, okay?"

Needless to say, I was determined to be Web's partner—especially since I was pretty sure we'd end up learning mouth-to-mouth at some point during the week. But he was sitting three spots away from me, which made my teaming up with him easier said than done.

I stared over at him, but he was still looking up at Mr. Whittle. Around me, I saw other counselors turning Web's way, so I knew I'd have to act fast.

I turned my whole body toward Web, being careful to avoid eye contact with anyone who wasn't him. He was sure to look my way eventually, but by then it might be too late. All around me, the other counselors were already talking and pairing up.

Casually, I stood up, still keeping my eyes locked only on him. If nothing else, my standing might draw his attention.

Sure enough, I saw his head turn, and our eyes met at last. He smiled.

And then Min stepped right in front of me, blocking Web completely, like the moon blotting out the sun. She'd stood up too. Min and I looked at each other, and for a second I thought she was going to ask me to be her partner, despite what Mr. Whittle had said about not pairing up with people we knew.

But then, without a word, Min turned toward Web. Even though she was facing away from me, I heard her say to him, clear as a bell, "Hey, you got a partner?"

"No," he said, his voice still all milk and honey. "Let's do it."

In other words, Min ended up as Web's partner, not me. And I wanted to wring her damn neck.

I still needed a partner, but now I didn't care who it turned out to be.

A voice next to me said, "You paired up yet?"

I looked. It was this kid with a big scar that

covered the left half of his face, which I'm reluctant to mention because it makes it sound like this was his defining characteristic when it shouldn't be (sort of like Min being Chinese-American). Then again, that scar *was* this kid's defining characteristic, at least looks-wise. Somehow it makes me seem like less of a jerk if I also say he had brown hair.

"No," I said, meaning I wasn't paired up yet. I made a point of smiling at him. "But I guess I got a partner now, huh? Russel Middlebrook."

"Otto Digmore," he said. He didn't hold out his hand for a handshake or anything geeky like that.

"Great name," I said.

I wasn't being sarcastic, but Otto just rolled his eyes and said, "Yeah, just what I need, right?" He laughed, and I laughed too, even though it seemed like our laughter had something to do with his scar, and that made me uncomfortable.

All around us, the various teams of counselors were introducing themselves to each other. I wondered what Min was saying to Web. Even more, I wondered what he was saying to her. I tried to listen.

"So," Otto said to me, "why'd you want to be

a camp counselor?"

"Huh?" I said. "I don't know. Just wanted to get away, I guess."

"From what?"

It wasn't like I could tell him the truth. So I said, "Parents," and he nodded knowingly. "You?"

"I was a counselor last year."

"Yeah?" I said. "Like it?"

He shrugged. "I guess. I've been coming back for as long as I can remember. I used to go to camp here myself."

Talking to Otto, I found it impossible not to look at his scar. It was darker than the rest of his skin, with faint brown streaks. It was probably a skin graft, I decided—a patch job on some really serious burn. But from the look of things, it had happened a long time ago. The scar had sort of a swirl pattern to it, and it almost looked like his whole face was being sucked down a drain. And in the middle of all the scar tissue, where the drain would be, was his eye. It reminded me of the eye of a whale—obviously intelligent, yet peering out from behind something thick and rough and alien. (I immediately felt guilty for thinking this.)

It was one thing to notice the scar on Otto's

face; it was another thing to let him know I was noticing. So I said, "You must know what Whittle is going to have us do this week, right?"

He nodded. "Mostly just a lot of talk. You know—camp rules and regulations. And what to do if a kid gets a stomachache, stuff like that."

That didn't sound like we counselors would be getting all that cozy, I thought. Maybe it didn't matter that Web had ended up as Min's partner and not mine.

"And sometime this week," Otto went on, "we'll probably have to learn first aid and lifesaving and mouth-to-mouth."

*I hate you, Min!* I wanted to shout. Frowning, I glanced over at her, but she didn't even notice. She was too busy talking to Web—intensely, I might add. She was the one who'd been encouraging me to notice hot guys. But now that I'd noticed one, she'd stepped right in and taken him from me. It was almost like she'd done it on purpose.

A moment later, I realized that Otto was looking at me like he'd asked a question. I guess I'd been so busy scowling at Min that I hadn't been listening.

"Huh?" I said.

"Nothing," he said. He was looking at his

feet. The hair on the top of his head was so thick that I couldn't see the scalp, and I wondered if it was some kind of artificial weave. Maybe the burn he'd been in had taken off part of his hair too.

"Sorry, that was rude," I said. "What'd you ask?"

Otto shrugged. "I just wanted to know if you ever went to summer camp."

"Day camp," I said. "Does that count?"

"Oh, it's not the same thing at all."

"Yeah? Why not?"

"Something about spending the night. Things happen."

"Like what?"

"Ever hear of camp stew?" Otto asked.

I shook my head no.

"It's when the cook takes all the leftovers from the previous week and mixes them together into one big mess. It's absolutely disgusting. Last year, anyone who ate a whole portion got double dessert. Did they ever do *that* at day camp?"

"Uh," I said, "I don't think so."

"And the pranks! You know, you don't really know how to make a bed until you first learn the art of short-sheeting one!"

I smiled while Otto went on talking. He was

funny and interesting. He wasn't Web, but maybe he was the next best thing.

Two days later, we'd learned CPR, first aid, lifesaving, and yes, mouth-to-mouth, not to mention about a thousand camp rules and regulations, none of which I will bore you with here. I'd also spoken a grand total of six sentences directly to Web Bastian. On the plus side, I'd only sounded like a blithering idiot twice.

Wednesday night, just before lights-out, I was walking from the bathroom back to the cabin where all the guy counselors were sleeping when I heard a sneeze in the dark.

"Gesundheit!" I said, even though I had no idea who I was saying it to. Who knows? I thought. Maybe it's Web.

"Thanks," said a voice. It wasn't Web. It was a girl.

I pointed the beam of my flashlight toward the sound and accidentally flashed it right in the face of one of the other counselors. Her name was Em. She had a flashlight too and must have been walking to or from the bathroom herself.

"Oh!" I said, quickly lowering the flashlight. "Sorry."

" 'Sokay," she said, blowing her nose in a Kleenex. "Hay fever. Real smart idea to sign up as a camp counselor, huh?"

I smiled. Em had straight brown hair and round tortoiseshell glasses, like some kind of female Harry Potter. I'd spent the last two days sitting near her, but we hadn't talked about anything except camp stuff. She was sort of gawky, but I liked what I'd seen of her. She was the type of person who played Dungeons & Dragons, and who wouldn't be caught dead in a tanning booth.

"You know what's making you sneeze?" I asked. All I smelled was pine trees and dirt.

*"Thuja plicata,"* Em said.

"Huh?"

"That's what I'm allergic to. Also known as western red cedar. It's the tree pollen."

"You know the scientific name of red cedar?" What was it with people suddenly knowing the scientific names of things? Was I not paying attention in biology, or what?

Em blew her nose again. "No. Actually, I just made that up."

"Really?"

"No. I was lying before. That really is its scientific name."

By now, I was thoroughly confused. But I have to admit I was also entertained. I chuckled.

"So I'm Em," she said. "But you know that already, don't you? Just like I know that you're Russel. Or is it Russ?"

"Most people call me Russel. Does anyone call you Emily?"

"Actually, Em is short for Emeraldine."

"Really?"

"No, I'm lying again."

This time, I laughed out loud.

"So what do you think so far?" Em asked.

"Of camp? Oh, it's great. I really needed to get away."

"Yeah? From what?"

I decided then and there that I needed to stop telling people this.

"Parents," I said. "Why'd you come?"

"My sister's getting married in August. And she was hard enough to take *before* she started obsessing about the difference between almonds and pecans in her groom's cake."

I liked this girl's attitude. Which meant I also liked her.

Suddenly, someone coughed. It sounded like it was coming from the guy counselors' cabin. It sounded like Web.

"Well," I said. "I should probably get back. Nice to 'meet' you."

"Likewise," Em said. "Oh, and Russel?"

I glanced back at her—only to see her shine the beam of her flashlight right into my eyes.

The next morning—Thursday—the camp director gathered us in the lodge's common room like always (and, like always, Web looked *Teen People* cute!). But this time, Mr. Whittle had two new adults with him—a man and a woman—and they both had big burn scars on their faces, like Otto. (Incidentally, one other counselor, a girl named Janelle, had facial scars too, but they weren't as bad as Otto's.)

"Every June, Camp Serenity becomes a very special place," Mr. Whittle said in this hushed, somber tone that annoyed me somehow. "That's because we reserve our first two-week session for a particular group of kids. These are kids who might not feel comfortable at our other sessions or at other summer camps, okay? Most are burn survivors with scars or kids who have other facial injuries." I remembered, now, that Mr. Whittle had explained all this during my job interview, but I'd mostly pushed it out of my mind. Of course, this explained the scars on Otto's and Janelle's faces. Otto must have started coming to Camp Serenity as a burn survivor and stayed on as a counselor. But I didn't see how any of this made much of a difference to anything, which is why I'm only getting around to mentioning it now.

"Anyway," Mr. Whittle went on, "Ryan and Jean here are burn survivors themselves, and they're also going to be our guests for the first two weeks of camp. And for the next two days, they're going to help us prepare for the arrival of our first session of kids, okay?"

So we were going to get burn survivor sensitivity training, I thought to myself. I guess that made sense. Except for Otto, I didn't have any experience with people who'd been burned. I sure as hell didn't want to say or do the wrong thing.

"Thanks, Al," Jean said to Mr. Whittle. She stood up and looked around at us all. She didn't say anything, just smiled. Now, there are smiles, and there are *smiles*. Her whole face lit up. Jean's grin wasn't just disarming; it was a goddamn political statement. It was like two guys walking down the street holding hands—you're going to notice whether you like it or not. I'm beautiful and I'm happy, Jean told us with that smile. And the amazing thing was, you totally believed her.

Finally, Jean said, "How many of you here went to summer camp?"

Eight out of the ten counselors raised their hands—including me (unlike Otto, I figured day camp *did* count).

"And what was it you liked best?" Jean asked.

"The canoes," Min said.

"Roasting marshmallows around the campfire," a counselor named Lorna said.

"Archery," Web said.

"The chocolate chip pancakes," Em said, and everyone laughed.

I tried to think of something to say, but couldn't remember anything in particular. (All right, I thought, so maybe day camp *didn't* count.)

As each of us spoke up, Jean kept grinning like a Cheshire cat. Finally, she said, "Fantastic! Well, you know what? Those are all the things we want our kids to remember about camp too!" She thought for a second, then winked at Em. "I'll see what we can do about the chocolate chip pancakes." We all laughed again. Then Jean got serious. "But sometimes something as simple as a couple of weeks at summer camp can be a horrible experience for a burn survivor. That's because kids with scars on their faces are sometimes made to feel like they don't fit in with kids who don't have scars."

And so began two days of burn survivor sensitivity training. It was pretty basic stuff. For example, Ryan said, "We're burn 'survivors,' not burn 'victims.' No one wants to be known as a 'victim' their whole life, right?"

But the biggest lesson, one we heard again and again, was that burn survivors wanted people to see beyond their scars. They didn't want to be defined by their injuries. They wanted to be seen as individuals, just like anyone else.

"Burn survivors are used to being treated like freaks and monsters," Jean told us. "But we're not monsters. And over the course of the next two weeks, it's your job and mine to make sure that none of these kids feel like monsters either. For them, this is a chance to have two weeks where they can completely forget about what they look like on the outside."

I listened attentively to all this, and I contributed during the group discussions. But the truth was, I didn't think any of it applied to me.

After all, I was gay. I knew all about what it was like to be stereotyped—to have people assume lots of negative things about me, and to make all these snap judgments. I sure wasn't about to do stuff like that to anyone else. I'd treated Otto like an individual, hadn't I? (Even if his eye *had* reminded me of a whale's.)

Saturday was our day off; then Sunday came. Counselor orientation was over, and the burn survivors finally arrived. Unfortunately, it took me less than an hour to learn that Jean and Ryan were absolutely wrong: these burn survivor kids *were* monsters. Only it had nothing whatsoever to do with the way they looked.

# Chapter Three

I was standing in the middle of a raging hurricane. The fury of the storm battered and bewildered me.

Okay, so it wasn't a real hurricane. I'm doing that thing I did when I said the school hallway was on fire, when I tried to fool you into thinking one thing, only to spring on you that I meant something else entirely. In this case, I'm talking about my campers, who I now realize I also just compared to monsters. I am aware this is bringing me dangerously close to metaphor overload, so let's just get to the point, shall we?

My campers were out of control. Each of us counselors had been assigned a cabin of eight kids. They'd been grouped by age and gender, and I had eight ten-year-old boys. By the time we got to our cabin, they were reminding me of Helen Keller in that play

*The Miracle Worker*, but before Anne Sullivan turns the wild, shrieking Helen into a halfway-normal human being. I'm exaggerating, but only a little.

Mr. Whittle had divided up the kids out on the marching field, separating them into their various cabin groups. That part went okay, I guess because the kids were all still kind of stunned to realize they'd really be away from home for the next two weeks and because Mr. Whittle and Jean and Ryan were standing right there.

Out on that marching field, I'd introduced myself to my campers as their counselor and asked them their names.

No one said anything. At this point, they actually seemed kind of shy. This was probably the first time many of them had ever been away from their parents for more than a day or so.

"You," I said, pointing to the closest kid. "What's your name?"

I'd happened to pick the one kid who didn't seem shy at all. In fact, as I looked at him, he glared back at me the way a lion looks at a gazelle—like he hated me in some primal, instinctive way. He obviously resented being here and was now determined to take it out on me. But finally, through gritted teeth, he spoke his name: "Ian."

Now that I was looking right at him, I saw that I'd also picked the kid with the least obvious facial scars. Up close, you could see that his skin almost looked like it had melted a little, but from farther back, he just looked slightly out of focus. Anyway, I couldn't help but wonder if the other kids had noticed that I'd called on Ian first—that maybe I thought he was special because he didn't look so bad.

"All right," I said. I quickly pointed to another random kid. "You?"

"Zach," the other kid said. And that's when I realized that I'd gone from the kid with the least obvious injuries to the one with the most obvious ones. A lot of Zach's body was covered with this white, gauzelike clothing. A few days earlier, I'd learned that this was something called a pressure garment and that it helped with the healing. Zach also had this white plastic mask over his face, which was kind of disturbing, with his eyes peering out and everything. It made him look a little like the Phantom of the Opera (I was sure he was very sick of hearing *that*!).

"Okay," I said, picking out another kid. "You?"

"Trevor," said a kid with a facial scar that reminded me a little of a seahorse.

And so we went on down the line—to Willy,

Noah, Kwame, Julian, and Blake—and I decided that burn survivors are like snowflakes: no two are exactly alike. They had big scars, little scars, dark scars, light scars, pressure garments or bandages, and no pressure garments or bandages. (There were also kids in wheelchairs and on crutches, but I didn't have any of those. They were staying in the main lodge with Jean and Ryan as their counselors.) One of my kids—Julian—wasn't even a burn survivor. He just had the worst case of zits I'd ever seen. (I later learned this was something called early-onset acne conglobata.)

In short, we weren't exactly the Brady Bunch. But I'd had my two days of burn survivor training, right? Plus I was gay and oh-so-sensitive.

With the introductions over, I led my kids to our cabin so they could unpack. And this was where things started to go seriously wrong. In the mere two hundred yards between the marching field and our cabin, something had happened to my kids. It had to do with the fact that they were all burn survivors. Around other kids like themselves, it suddenly didn't matter what any of them looked like on the outside, just like Jean had said. So now, in a way, they *weren't* burn survivors. Now they were just ten-year-old boys.

Hyperactive ten-year-old boys.

Hyperactive ten-year-old boys who were suddenly fast friends.

Or maybe "friends" is the wrong word. Maybe they'd just become united in their opposition to me—who, incidentally, was *not* a burn survivor, and so was suddenly the odd guy out.

Anyway, by the time we reached the cabin, they were running all over the place, laughing and playing.

"All right!" I said. "Settle down, okay?" My whole life, I'd been hearing teachers say this to kids. It felt bizarre for me to be the one saying it now.

I got the same reaction that most of my teachers got. No one paid any attention.

Okay, so maybe their running around and playing wasn't the worst thing in the world. (How often did *these* kids get a chance to play like that, anyway?) But then the kid with the out-of-focus face started climbing to the top of one of the bunks. Once at the top, he turned around like he was going to jump down onto one of the single beds below.

"Hey!" I said. "You there, don't do that!" By this point, I had already forgotten all their names.

Of course, the kid jumped anyway, landing with a big squeak.

Three kids immediately veered for the bunk bed and started climbing.

"Stop!" I said. "Everyone just stop right now!"

Still everyone ignored me. The three kids kept climbing up the bunk, and one of the other kids pulled a squirt gun out of his bag, pointed it at me, and fired. He'd actually come to camp with the damn thing already filled with water.

What gave here? This wasn't what I'd expected at all. These kids were burn survivors, so I guess I'd expected them to be all nervous and noble and shy, like disabled kids always are in TV movies. I hadn't counted on the ten-year-old boy thing.

As I stood there, helplessly watching my kids go berserk, I realized two things. The first was that Trevor (whose name, at this point, I still couldn't remember) wasn't really joining in. He was just watching the other kids, looking nervous and noble and shy, like *all* these kids were supposed to look. The second thing I realized was that out-of-focus Ian (whose name I also couldn't remember) was egging the other kids on. Somehow, he was in the center of all this mayhem, controlling the other kids like a cop directing traffic. If this really had been a hurricane, he would have been the eye—the dead calm at the center of the storm. Which was funny, because I figured if anyone had a reason to be anti-social, it was Zach, the kid with the pressure garment and face mask (oops—pity alert!).

I decided that if I was ever going to get my kids in order again, I'd need to go to the root of the problem—namely, Ian. But how? I didn't feel right about just reaching out and grabbing him. And I didn't want to embarrass him in front of his new friends—hadn't he been embarrassed enough already? So I said, as calmly as possible, "Ian? Can I see you outside for a second?"

He was just pulling a can of shaving cream out of his duffel bag (and I was pretty sure he wasn't going to use it to shave). He also completely ignored me.

Screw this, I thought. What was I doing there? Why in the world had I thought that being a camp counselor was a good way to spend my summer? R&R? *Ha!* I saw now that being a camp counselor was just another form of baby-sitting, but without the fresh DVDs and well-stocked refrigerator.

I didn't need this. I could walk away right then and there. I could say I wasn't feeling well, that I was homesick, that I wasn't comfortable working with burn survivors. True, I'd signed a contract with Mr. Whittle saying I'd work the whole summer, but it wasn't legally binding (the one good thing about being sixteen years old!). True, I wouldn't see Gunnar and Min all summer long, but it wasn't like I had no other friends.

I turned to look out the open door, to a world of freedom without shrieking kids.

And at that exact moment, Web walked by outside, leading his kids on the way to their cabin. He had the eleven-year-old boys, and they were all walking in single file, like they were thrilled just to be following in his footsteps.

Web looked over at me and nodded. I nodded back—pretty damn confidently, if I do say so myself. From where he was, he couldn't see the chaos inside my cabin—which was a good thing, because I sure didn't want him thinking I couldn't handle eight ten-year-old boys.

I can't leave camp, I thought to myself. True, my contract with Mr. Whittle wasn't legally binding, but there was no way he was going to let me just walk away, especially after five full days of training. Besides, I'd made a commitment—to Gunnar, to Ryan and Jean, even to Mr. Whittle. Plus I had no ride home.

Oh, hell, I admit it. I was completely infatuated with Web. He was the reason I couldn't leave.

I took a deep breath, steeling myself for another skirmish with my charges.

And at that exact moment, Ian came up behind me and jerked down my shorts, exposing my white briefs for the whole world to see—including Web, who was still looking right at me.

I somehow managed to get my kids through dinner (which was slightly less insane, if only because adults were around), and then through lights-out (don't get me started). Once I was sure all the kids were asleep, I left to meet Min and Gunnar. We'd agreed to rendezvous that night at this sheltered little cove a few minutes' walk north of camp. We'd accidentally discovered it when we were out exploring the week before. Eventually, the other counselors would probably discover it too, but for the time being it was our own secret hideaway.

"Oh. My. God." This was me. It was the first thing I said to my two friends. They were lounging on this big granite boulder that extended from the beach out into the water. I have no idea what the Rock of Gibraltar looks like, but let's say it looked like that.

"What?" Gunnar said to me.

"Are you kidding?" I said, climbing up onto the rock to join them. "They're a bunch of *brats*! And when they're not running around shrieking, they're puking!" I wasn't exaggerating. Immediately after arriving back at the cabin after dinner, Willy had thrown up, probably as a result of all the excitement of the day. The smell had resulted in a vomit chain reaction in which Julian and Kwame had proceeded to throw up too. No one—I repeat, *no one!*—had managed to make it ten feet to the outside of the cabin.

"Your kids?" Gunnar asked.

"Yes, my kids! They are out of control! Aren't yours?"

"Not really. I guess I got lucky. I think I got the nerds."

"And mine are nine-year-old girls," Min said. "In two years, they'll be all snooty and premenstrual, but for the time being, they're just sparkle nail polish and Bratz Slumber Party."

All my life, I'd thought that when a class was out of control, it was all the teacher's fault. I remembered so many teachers snidely saying how this class or that one was just so "difficult," and I'd always chalked it up to their making excuses for their own pathetic teaching. But now I saw that they weren't just making excuses, that there really was something to the idea that not every group of kids is the same.

"So," Gunnar said to me, "you probably regret coming here, huh? You wanna go home?"

Now I'd done it. I'd made Gunnar feel bad. After all, this whole camp thing had been his idea. One more reason I couldn't just vacate in disgust.

"Oh, it's not that bad," I said, backpedaling. "I just need to get a grip." I was still trying to find a place to sit on the rock. The top was uneven, and Min and Gunnar had taken the only two flat spots.

"What about the other counselors?" Min said, sipping on a Diet Coke. "What do we think about them by now?"

"I like Em," I said. "I think she's great."

"Oh, yeah," Min said. "Em's great."

"And Otto," I said. "He seems nice."

"I like Otto too," Min said. "Anyone else?"

"Well," I said, finally finding a decent place to sit, "there's always Web."

"What about him?" Gunnar asked. My straight best friend—clueless to the end.

I decided to spell it all out for Gunnar. "I like him," I said.

"Web?" Min said dubiously. "Really?"

"Are you kidding?" I said. "Have you *seen* him?"

"Huh," Gunnar said. "I wouldn't figure you'd go for the 'bad boy' type."

"'Bad boy'!" I said. "Web's not a 'bad boy'!"

Gunnar rolled his eyes. "Are you kidding? He definitely is."

As much as I hated to admit it, my straight best

friend wasn't quite as clueless as I'd thought. Did I go for the "bad boy" type? The only other guy I'd ever been hot for was this baseball player from our school, and he'd been dark and butch and kind of cocky. In short, a "bad boy" (but a *nice* "bad boy"!).

I looked over at Min. "What do you know about him?"

Min was staring out at the darkening lake. "Web?" she said. "Not much."

"Come on! You were his partner the whole last week. Thanks a lot for that, by the way."

"I do know one thing," Min said. "He's not gay."

This wasn't what I was wanting to hear.

"How do you know?" I asked Min.

"He had a girlfriend," she said.

"That doesn't mean anything," I said. "Maybe he's just not out. Maybe he hasn't figured it out yet. Or maybe he's bisexual. You of all people should know that just because he has a girlfriend, that doesn't mean he's not gay!"

"It's a feeling, then," Min said. "He's not gay, I can tell. Gaydar."

"You can't have gaydar!" I said. "You're bi!" Yes, I know this was a dumb thing to say, but I was desperate. I really wanted there to be some way for me to hook up with Web.

"Russel," Min said evenly. "Trust me. He's not gay."

I wasn't sure why Min was pissing me off—she was just giving her opinion, right? But she was really making me mad.

"He *might* be gay," I said, barely able to keep my balance on the rock.

"He's not!" Min said, so loudly that it echoed in the little cove.

In the silence that followed, waves lapped against the rock, which was weird because the water had been calm before and I hadn't heard any boats go by.

"So what's up with Mr. Whittle's nose hair?" Gunnar said, obviously changing the subject on purpose. "Does it drive you guys as crazy as it does me?"

I didn't say anything, and Min didn't either. She shifted uncomfortably, but I don't think it had anything to do with the uneven surface of the rock.

"Min," I said softly, "it doesn't matter what Web is. I just think he's cute."

She looked over at me. "He's not gay."

Okay, now I was annoyed. Here I'd been all mature, trying to move on and everything, and she wouldn't let it rest.

"You don't know that!" I said. "There's no way you can possibly know if he's gay or not!"

"Who cares?" Gunnar said. "What difference does it make who's gay?"

This was a good question. Why *did* Min care so much? She had always had a competitive streak, especially with me. And a few months before, we'd both broken up with people at almost the same time. Did she not want me finding someone new before she did?

Suddenly, Min stood up. "I need to go check on my kids."

She hopped back down to the beach, but before she disappeared into the darkness, I couldn't resist saying, "He *could* be gay!" I know it was snotty, but Min had been being bitchy, and she'd been bitchy before I'd been snotty. Besides, I *was* only sixteen years old.

She turned around to face me.

"He's not gay," she said, neither bitchy nor snotty, but like she was just stating a scientific fact.

Frankly, it sounded to me like a dare.

## Chapter Four

**The** next day, the real camp schedule began. In the morning, the kids all got to pick an "individual activity" for the week, like woodworking or kayaking. For this they divided up into activity groups, each of which was led by a team of two counselors, and sometimes an adult. For the first week, I had arts and crafts (how gay is *that*?). It·went okay, probably because it was twelve girls and Blake, the least monster-y of my kids, after Trevor. Unfortunately, then I had to meet up with all my kids together, first for lunch, then for our daily "all-camp activity" (that day, it was sack races and tug-of-war on the marching field). As expected, my kids were little hurricane-monsters again, and there didn't seem to be anything I could do to control·them.

After that, the kids had a couple of hours of free time until dinner, but we counselors didn't get a break, because we still had to supervise them. I had lifeguard duty with Em down at the swimming area.

"Hey," I said, joining her on the beach. Neither of us bothered sitting in the actual lifeguard's chair, which was unbelievably uncomfortable. "How are the allergies?"

"I'm fine with the tree pollen," she said. "I just didn't know I'm also allergic to eleven-year-old girls."

"What do you mean?" It sounded like Em was having a hard time with her campers too, but I wasn't about to come right out and say what I really thought, not after the lackluster response from Min and Gunnar the night before.

She looked at me, sitting next to her on the sand. "They're little shits."

"Your kids?"

"Yup."

"Really?"

"Oh, please. I never would've gotten them to sleep last night if I hadn't put valerian root in their hot chocolate." Valerian root is this herbal supplement that puts people out.

"You didn't really!" I said. "Did you?"

"Yeah, I did."

**44**

"Really?"

"No, not really. I'm lying."

"Oh. Wait. Which is it?"

"I did it. I was telling the truth the first time. I was lying when I said I didn't do it."

My head was swimming—which I now realized was pretty typical when you were talking to Em.

I laughed. "So you really think your kids are . . . ?"

"Little shits?" Em said. "Abso-frickin'-lutely. Aren't yours? They sure looked like it at lunch."

"Well, yeah, but . . ." But what? My campers *were* little shits. It just felt funny saying that out loud. Them being burn survivors and all.

"So say it," Em said.

"What?"

"Say your kids are little shits!"

I laughed again. That's when I realized something about Em. She reminded me of Gunnar. She had the same kind of quirky nature where you were never quite sure what she was going to say next. Plus they both knew the scientific names of things.

Suddenly, Ian stepped up next to me on the beach. He jammed his foot down into the sand, which happened to be right where my tube of sunblock was sitting. It was uncapped, so white sunblock squirted out, gooping up my leg.

"Oops," he said. "Sorry." He wasn't sorry at all. He'd done it on purpose. But I would have felt weird yelling at him. What exactly was I going to say?

But Em didn't hesitate. As Ian was turning away, she stuck her foot out right in front of him. He tripped and went sprawling over the sand.

"Oops!" she said to him. "Sorry."

I admit it. Now I *really* liked Em.

For one hour every afternoon, we counselors were supposed to take turns operating the camp store, located in a tiny room in the lodge, just off the cafeteria. Basically, it sold candy, soda pop, a few toys, some clothing, and toiletries like toothpaste that eighty percent of the kids had left at home. I knew Gunnar was in the camp store that first week, so I visited him on a break from lifeguarding.

"Hey," I said.

"Huh? Oh, hey, Russ." He'd been reading a paperback, and even though he tried to hide the cover with his arm, I caught a glimpse of a bare-chested man embracing a woman in a frilly dress. Strange, I thought: Gunnar was reading a romance novel. But I decided not to embarrass him by pointing that out.

Instead, I put a dollar on the counter and reached for a candy bar. But Gunnar said, "You don't want that."

"Why not?" I said.

"Because it's not fit for human consumption."

"Why not?"

"Four words: hydrogenated palm kernel oil."

"Hydrogenated what?"

"It's real nasty stuff," Gunnar said. "They take this cheap vegetable oil and add an extra hydrogen atom to make it stiff. It sticks right to your arteries. It's even worse than hardened bacon grease."

"Fine," I said. "I'll have one of these." I reached for a different candy bar.

Gunnar still wouldn't take my money. "Oh, no, there's palm kernel oil in almost everything these days. At least all the cheap stuff."

"Whatever," I said. "Just give me a can of pop."

He stared at me with a disgusted look on his face.

"Now what?" I said.

"You know they don't even use sugar in pop anymore? They use this stuff called high-fructose corn syrup. It's made out of corn, but it's completely unnatural. Our bodies have no way to handle it. It's one of the reasons why Americans have gotten so fat."

"Uh-huh," I said. "You know, your salesmanship skills leave something to be desired."

"Hey, I'm only looking out for your health."

I decided to change the subject. "I wanted to ask you something. What do you think of Em?" The wheels in my head had been turning. I figured Gunnar wanted a girlfriend and Em reminded me of him, so why not try to hook the two of them up?

But Gunnar wasn't ready to switch topics. "If you're hungry and you want my advice, go get an apple from the kitchen. The corporations still haven't figured out a way to screw up a piece of fruit. Well, except for the pesticides. Be sure and wash it good."

"Fine," I said. "But I still want to know what you think of Em."

"The counselor? She's okay."

"I really like her."

"Do you realize there's not a single healthy food item in the whole camp store?" Gunnar said. "I mean, would you look at the ingredients in these Doritos?"

"I think you'd like her too," I said.

I had Gunnar's attention at last. "Wait a minute. I know what you're doing."

"What am I doing?"

"You're doing the matchmaker thing!"

"What? No, I'm not."

"Yes, you are! Why else would you care what

I thought of Em?"

Gunnar had me. I figured I might as well come clean. "Well, so what if I am?"

"So I already told you! I'm giving up girls!"

"You were *serious* about that?"

"Darn right. Russ, you've been there all these years. You know how I am around girls. I always screw it up. It's humiliating."

"Well, yeah, but—"

"There is no 'but.'" He thought for a second, then said, "Do you remember when I asked my parents for that theremin for Christmas?"

A theremin is an electronic instrument that you play by moving your hands around these two metal antennas. It makes the weird *woo-woo* sound you hear in old science fiction movies.

"I remember," I said.

"I'd never wanted anything so much as I wanted that theremin. And do you remember what happened that Christmas?"

"You didn't get it."

He nodded. "My parents got me a synthesizer instead. They said the music shop said that a synthesizer could do everything that a theremin could do, plus other stuff. I'd never been so disappointed in my entire life."

"Gunnar," I said, "what does this have to do with—?"

"I'd dreamed about that theremin for *months*. And I didn't get it! I couldn't afford to buy one myself, and it was forever until my birthday. I couldn't bear the thought of wanting anything that bad for so long again. And what if I asked for it for my birthday and my parents got me a xylophone? I knew I wouldn't have been able to handle that disappointment. So I made myself stop wanting that theremin. I *willed* myself to not want it. And I did."

"No, you didn't!" I said. "I see your face every time we hear a theremin in a movie or whatever."

"Yes, I did!" Gunnar said firmly. "And it's the same thing with my wanting a girlfriend. I don't want to be disappointed by not getting the girl ever again. And now I won't be."

"Gunnar—"

But at that exact moment, a couple of kids barged into the camp store.

"We'll talk about this later," I said. It was time for me to get back to lifeguarding, anyway.

"There's nothing to talk about!" Gunnar said. Then he turned his attention to the kids, who were already reaching for candy bars.

"You don't want that," I heard him say.

\* \* \*

The good news was that none of my kids threw up that night. The bad news was that I almost did. Almost every one of my kids had some salve or ointment that he had to put on at night (even Julian had zit cream). Most of those ointments smelled strong enough by themselves. All together, it was like sleeping in a medicine chest. But I sure as hell couldn't *say* anything. It wasn't like it was these kids' fault that they had to put on all those creams.

Still, I was plenty happy when the kids were finally all asleep and I could get out into the fresh night air. I knew the other counselors were gathering around the fire pit on the beach, so I went down to join them.

I saw Min sitting on one side of the campfire and I thought about sitting next to her, but I was still a little peeved by the way she'd acted the night before. So I decided to sit next to Otto instead. I'd seen him around, but I hadn't really talked to him since he'd been my partner during counselor orientation.

"How's it going?" I said, plunking down next to him.

"Oh!" he said. "Good! You want a marshmallow?" He and the other counselors were roasting them over the fire.

"Sure," I said. "Thanks."

"Here, you can use my stick."

I took the stick, poked a marshmallow with it, and aimed it at the fire. The other counselors were having little conversations all around us, but I couldn't think of anything else to say to Otto.

"So what do you think so far?" he asked.

"Of camp?" I said. "Well, you didn't tell me they'd keep us this busy."

"It gets easier. The kids are just testing you."

"I guess."

"What?" he said.

I shrugged. "I don't know. I just don't think I'm very good at this counselor thing."

"Can I give you some advice?"

"Huh? Oh, yeah. Sure."

"It's just that I was watching you at lunch." What in the world? Had the whole camp been watching me and my kids at lunch or what?

"I kind of think you're letting them walk all over you," Otto went on.

"I guess," I said. "I just hate to yell at them." I checked my marshmallow, but it wasn't even singed. I was still too far from the fire, so I stuck my stick farther in.

"Why?" Otto asked.

"Why what?"

"Why do you hate to yell at 'em?"

"Oh, I don't know." Okay, so this was really awkward. I didn't want to yell at them because they were burn survivors. But I didn't want to say that to Otto, who was a burn survivor himself.

"It's okay, you know. They won't break."

"What?" I said, fiddling with my stick. "You mean my kids?"

"Sure. Remember what Jean and Ryan said? Burn survivors just want to be treated like everyone else. Maybe your kids can tell that you're nervous around them."

"But—"

"What?"

I couldn't think of anything to say. Which told me Otto was right. I felt like I couldn't come down on them. But just because you feel something, that doesn't mean it's right.

"So you think I should just go for it?" I said. "Be a real hard-ass?"

He laughed. "Within reason. You know, I think I'm the only kid in my whole school who loves it when teachers are hard on me. But I do, because then I know for a fact they aren't giving me special treatment. That they see me, not just my scar."

There was this kind of awkward silence. "So," I said, "you like it up here . . . ?" I'd been going to say "with your own kind," but I figured that sounded really stupid, especially given what he'd just said about people seeing beyond his scar. Fortunately, my abbreviated half sentence happened to sound like a complete sentence—like that's what I'd been going to say all along.

"Oh, sure," Otto said. "But I miss being home too."

"Yeah? Friends?"

"And parents. You?"

"Well, my two best friends are here. So I don't really miss anything." On the contrary, I thought. It was a relief to be away from a hometown where everyone was whispering behind my back. I didn't ever want to go back.

"No girlfriend?"

Girlfriend. Otto was asking me if I had a girlfriend. Which wasn't any big deal. Except that fully answering that question meant telling him that I didn't have a girlfriend and I didn't want one. That I was gay.

"No," I said. "No girlfriend." I couldn't do it. I couldn't tell him the truth. It's not like I was ashamed or anything. It's just that one of the reasons I'd come to this camp was to get away from being The Gay Kid for a few weeks. If I told Otto the truth, he might keep it a secret if I asked him to. Then again, he might not. He might tell the whole camp—and then I'd be right back where I'd been during the school year.

"Your marshmallow," Otto said.

"Huh?" I said.

"I think it's on fire."

I pulled my stick back from the campfire. Sure enough, the marshmallow was in flames. This time, I'd been too close to the fire.

"Here," he said, reaching for the bag. "Have another one."

"No," I said, standing. "I want to make sure my kids are still all asleep."

That night, before turning in, I stopped by the shower house to use the bathroom. I could hear water dripping in the room beyond the toilet area, like someone had taken a shower not long before.

I was washing my hands at the sink when a voice said, "I thought I heard someone out here."

I turned.

It was Web. He was standing in the doorway to the showers. And of course, the only thing he was wearing was a thin white towel around his waist.

Let's just say he had a great body. Broad shoulders, dark nipples, and just a little bit of dark hair on his upper chest and lean lower stomach. And it seems important to mention—and I'm fully aware that this might very well fall into the category of "too much information"—that there was a big bulge in the towel in the exact location of his you-know-what.

"Oh!" I said.

"Didn't mean to scare you."

"You didn't!" The fact that my pulse was pounding so hard had nothing whatsoever to do with the fact that he'd appeared so suddenly.

"So," he said casually. "What do you think?"

"Huh?" I said. I knew what I thought of his body, but that couldn't possibly be what he was asking me, could it?

"Of camp," he said. "You like it so far?"

"It's okay, I guess. I'm having some problems with—"

Web's hair and upper body were dripping wet, like I'd caught him right after he'd turned off the shower but before he'd had a chance to completely dry off. And it was right in the middle of my sentence that he nonchalantly slipped the towel from his body and started towel-drying his face and hair.

I didn't want to stare. The problem was, his face was completely covered by that towel, which meant I could look at his lower body with impunity. (Is that a word?) I admit it, the temptation was too great. His stomach was rippled, and the little trail of hair there led down to the deeper shadows below. And—again, I'm completely aware that this might be too much information!—"it" was even bigger than it had looked under the towel.

"What?" he said, completely innocently, from underneath the towel. "Problems with what?"

I turned away at last (even I have *some* ethics). "With my kids!" I said. "They're kind of bratty. Well, good night!"

He pulled the towel off his head. "You're going?"

"Yeah!" Moving backward, I bumped into a bathroom stall. Hard. It squeaked. Loudly. "Got to go check on my kids!" I couldn't believe I'd used the same lame excuse twice in one night.

"Okay," he said, turning toward the showers again and giving me a glimpse of the eighth Wonder of the World that was his perfectly rounded ass. "Good night."

" 'Night!" I said as I turned, fleeing out into it.

## Chapter Five

**For** the all-camp activity the following day, we went on a hike. Or rather, we went on ten separate hikes—a different one led by each of the camp's ten teenage counselors. We were all going in the same direction on the same trail—to the top of nearby Baldy Mountain, where we were supposed to meet for snacks. But that was all we had in common. Some of the counselors (mostly the guys) had turned it into a race, seeing which cabin could get to the top of the hill fastest; other counselors (mostly the girls) had turned it into a nature walk, identifying native plants to their campers and pointing out interesting land features along the way.

And then there was me, who was doing everything he could just to keep his kids moving in a forward direction.

First, we stopped to look at a snake swallowing a slug. Once someone had pointed it out, the kids all had to gather around it for a closer look.

"Okay," I said. "That's real interesting, but it's time to push on, okay?"

We did push on eventually, but not before the slug had completely disappeared into the snake's mouth.

A few minutes later, we stopped again when Willy spotted animal droppings alongside the trail.

"All right, all right," I said, noting to myself that even the girl cabins were quickly passing us by. "Let's keep moving, okay?"

We kept moving, but not because of what I'd said. No, it was because animal droppings are basically pretty boring.

Finally, we came to a flat wooden bridge built over a little pond.

"Cool!" Ian said, ignoring the bridge and heading down to the edge of the pond. This wouldn't have been a problem if we hadn't already stopped for the snake, the animal droppings, and everything else under the sun. When it came to the order of the various cabins hiking up the trail, we were now officially last.

"Wait a minute," I said. "Let's not stop again, okay?"

Ian looked back at me. "We're on a nature hike, right?" he said.

"Well, yeah, I guess," I said. "But—"

"And this pond is nature, right?"

"Well, yeah, but—"

"Then we can look at it." The other kids found his logic impeccable. (Is *that* a word?) So they all joined him at the edge of the pond.

"Hey!" Julian said. "Water skippers!"

Only now did I remember what Otto had told me the day before about treating my kids like any other kids. Just because they were burn survivors, I didn't have to put up with this crap.

"Okay, that's it!" I said. "It's time to go! I want everyone back on the trail right now!"

Ian glared at me. "Or what?" he said.

"What?" I said, taken aback.

"What are you going to do if we don't get back on the trail?"

I had to think about that. Mr. Whittle had given us counselors a couple of different disciplinary options: KP duty, or docking the kids some privilege, like s'mores around the campfire.

"I'll . . . ," I started to say, but it was too late. I'd hesitated. They say that he who hesitates is lost, and they're right. I'd hesitated. Ergo, I was lost. (I *know* "ergo" is a word! It means "therefore.")

Ian turned toward the undergrowth. "I hear a

stream," he said. He was speaking to his cabin mates like I didn't even exist. "Let's go check it out."

"No!" I said. "Don't go in there!"

But they were following Ian now, not me. I'd already used up all my ammunition—and I'd been firing blanks to begin with. So the kids followed Ian into the woods—even Trevor, who at least had the good grace to glance back at me guiltily before heading off into the woods.

"That's it!" I called after them. "No s'mores tonight!" In my defense, even as I said this I could hear how stupid it sounded.

Oh, boy, was I bad at this camp counselor thing or what?

"Fine," I said to myself, following after them. I couldn't very well have them walking into quicksand. (Or could I? It would sure solve a lot of my problems.)

But a mere ten yards from the trail, I noticed something about the undergrowth in front of me.

"Stop!" I shouted. "No one move!"

There must have been something in the urgency of my voice because—wonder of wonders—the kids actually stopped.

"Poison oak," I said. "It's all around you." Sure enough, there was even some of it growing between me and the kids.

"Poison *what?*" one of the kids said.

"It's really nasty stuff. It's got this oil on its leaves. If it touches your skin, you'll get a rash, and probably blisters. It really itches, and it takes forever to heal. And it doesn't even have to touch your skin. If it touches your clothes and then you touch them, the same thing happens."

I hadn't seen any poison oak around the camp grounds, which I guess is why Mr. Whittle hadn't issued any warnings. But had none of my kids ever seen the plant before? That seemed weird. Then I remembered that since this was a session for burn survivors, they'd come from all over the country. They must have all come from places where the plant never grew. (Had none of them ever even seen an oak tree? Because—duh!—poison oak looks a lot like oak. I think it was safe to say at this point that my cabin would not be winning the Camp Botany Award.)

When I was finished talking, the kids all looked at each other—and at Ian.

"Ignore him," he said. "He's lying."

"Fine," I said, like I couldn't have cared less (which was true). "When you guys get all covered with oozing blisters and spend the next four weeks going crazy trying not to scratch, don't come crying to me. Man, I just hope none of you already touched the stuff."

Nobody said anything. But they didn't move either. They just eyed the undergrowth around them like they were surrounded by hidden monsters, which I guess they kind of were.

And suddenly, I had a thought. I finally knew what Otto had been trying to tell me the night before. Burn survivors just wanted to be treated like any other kids? Well, I knew how I would treat any other kids in this exact same situation.

I started to turn away.

"Wait!" Blake said. "Where are you going?" There was actually a little fear in his voice.

"I'm getting the hell out of here," I said. "You guys sounded like you didn't want my help."

"Ian said that!" Blake said. "I didn't say that!"

I turned back to face the kids. I had their attention now, that's for sure. Even Ian was looking at me (while trying not to).

"You want my help?" I said.

Seven kids nodded emphatically.

"Fine," I said. "I'll show you what poison oak looks like. And I'll help you get back to the trail." I paused for just the right amount of time. "But only on one condition."

"What *condition*?" Ian said disdainfully. The kid had spunk, I had to give him that.

"Look," I said. "What's going on here is bull-shit, and you guys all know it. I'm your counselor, and you're just a bunch of ten-year-old kids. You want my help? You guys have to promise to do what I say for the rest of this session. I won't be a jerk, and you can still have fun. But when I say something is important, you have to listen. If so, I'll lead you out of the poison oak. If not, you're on your own."

"You wouldn't really leave us here!" Kwame said.

I laughed out loud. "You're kidding, right? Why wouldn't I leave you here? Serve you right, after the way you've been treating me."

I don't know if it was the tone of my voice or what. It might have been the laugh. But right then and there, I could have led those kids right off the Empire State Building. And they would have fol-lowed.

"He's bluffing," Ian said.

"Whatever," I said, turning for the trail again.

"Wait!" Trevor said, taking a step forward. "Take me with you!"

I shook my head. "Nope. All of you or none of you. You all chose to disobey me back there on the trail, so unless you all agree to listen to me now, you'll all suffer the consequences." I gave them a second to think over my terms. Then I said, "Well? What's your decision?"

Seven kids immediately vowed their undying obedience to me forever and ever.

I stared at the lone holdout. "Ian?"

"I still say you're bluffing," he said, but now he was the one who sounded pathetic, not me. "But okay," he added with a mumble.

"Okay what?" I said. "Say it." Yeah, I was rubbing it in. But it was Ian, so I figured I needed to have him spell it out.

"I'll do what you say until the end of the session!" he said, almost shouting.

"Good," I said quietly. And with that, I showed them what poison oak looks like, then turned and led them all to safety.

Believe it or not, that thing with the poison oak really seemed to make a difference. I won't say that my kids suddenly became little angels. But at least they followed behind me for the rest of the afternoon and mostly listened to what I had to say. We even made it to the top of Baldy Mountain, and we weren't the last cabin there either (that was the group led by Min, who could, unfortunately, be something of a know-it-all). I couldn't help but remember what Otto had told me about the kids wanting people to be strict with them because it meant they weren't getting special treatment as a result of their injuries.

That night, after lights-out, I was feeling pretty good about myself as I went down to join the other counselors around the campfire.

"What?" Gunnar said. He had noticed the self-satisfied look on my face.

"It just went well today with my kids," I said. "We were out on the hike, and they—"

Suddenly, someone started singing and playing the guitar on the other side of the campfire. It was Otto, playing this folksy ballad I'd never heard before, and I wondered if he'd written it himself.

*Is it okay if I need you tonight?*
*Thought I'd check and see if it's all right*
*'Cause the stars seem sort of far away,*
*the night is rather dark*
*Is it okay if I need you tonight?*

He was a good guitar player, not show-offy at all, but the kind who makes it look effortless. He barely had to move his hands and these complicated notes and rhythms came flowing out of the instrument.

But it was his voice that was the real wonder. Pure

and gentle, with just enough of an edge to keep it from being too saccharine. It was the voice of someone who had known both amazing joy and intense pain, and who knew that ultimately you can't really have one without the other. The secret of existence was all right there in his voice. He was breaking my heart—and making it sing!—at exactly the same time.

Gunnar heard it too. "Wow," he said—pretty much the perfect one-word description of Otto's music.

Otto sang:

> Don't get me wrong; I know tomorrow is
>     another day
> And I am strong. I'll survive whatever
>     comes my way
> But tonight the wind is howling, and I'm
>     chained out in the yard
> And for tonight being alone is just too hard

To tell the truth, Otto had such an amazing voice that it almost seemed to change the way he looked. How do I say this without sounding like a jerk? I'm not sure, so I'll just say it.

His singing almost made him look normal. It was the weirdest thing. Suddenly, I was seeing things about him that I'd never noticed before. His eyes, for example, which were the most unusual color—dark but warm, like burgundy or cherry wood. And his body, which was lean and tight, with great calves and even better forearms. As for the scar on his face, the more he sang, the more it seemed to melt away right before my eyes. Except that's not it, exactly. His scar wasn't *disappearing*. It just now seemed perfectly normal, not like a scar at all. If you'd asked me then and there, I would have sworn Otto was—well, beautiful.

> Is it okay if I want you tonight?
> It's a very long time until the morning light
> And since we're both here in the dark, can I
>     ask one thing of you?
> Is there any chance that you might want
>     me too?

"Hey, Russel," a voice said.

I didn't want to turn away, but I figured I had to.

"Huh?" I said, a little annoyed. But when I turned to look, I saw it wasn't Gunnar who'd been speaking. It was Web.

"Oh!" I said. "Hi!"

"Pretty good, huh?" Web was smiling when he said this, but he was looking at me, not Otto.

"What? Oh, yeah." Otto was still singing, but I

wasn't really listening anymore.

Web nodded back toward the cabins. "You wanna help me make rounds?" After lights-out, we counselors were supposed to go around and check on all the cabins once every hour until we turned in ourselves.

"Sure!" Usually, it was one guy and one girl who made the rounds, but I wasn't about to put up a fuss if it meant some alone time with Web.

I scrambled up from my seat on the ground—way too eagerly, I immediately realized. I thought I heard Otto's voice catch a little. I glanced over at him, but he was looking down at the sand.

"Let's go," Web said to me.

"Right!" I said, and we headed off together. Otto kept singing and playing, but his song didn't sound happy and sad anymore. Now it just sounded sad.

"Let's check the girls first," Web said, drawing my attention back to him.

"Okay," I said, and I swear, for the life of me, I couldn't think of one other thing to say. Our feet crunched on the gravel path up from the beach, which just made the silence seem even more awkward. Neither one of us had thought to bring our flashlights, so we were walking in total darkness. This late at night, there weren't even any lights coming from the lodge.

The girls' cabins were clustered in the trees along

the water on the south side of the camp. By the time we reached the first one, neither of us had managed another word.

We checked in on the five girls' cabins, but all the kids seemed to be sleeping soundly.

"Now the guys?" he said.

"Yeah," I said.

And so we headed back across the grass between the lodge and the beach. I still couldn't see Web, but it was impossible to forget he was there. Walking next to me on that grass, he was like a black hole, sucking every ounce of energy right out of my body.

Suddenly, Web said, "Hey! Look!"

I could tell he had stopped walking, but I wasn't sure where he was in the dark, or what he was talking about. So I said, "Huh?"

"The stars! I can see Leo."

I looked up into the sky. This far from the city lights, the stars were brighter than I'd ever seen them. The sky looked like the photo negative of a vast sandy beach. "Where?" I asked.

A darkened silhouette pointed up into the dome of stars. "There."

I didn't say anything, mostly because I still couldn't see where he was pointing.

Web laughed. "Here," he said, stepping close to

me—*behind* me. I couldn't see him, but suddenly I could sure feel him. From behind, he was guiding me by the biceps with one hand and resting his other arm on my shoulder, pointing it—and me—in the right direction. "There," he whispered, and I could feel his breath on the back of my neck. (The night was warm, but I shivered.) "See it? That sort of upside-down question mark? That's the head. And those other five stars? That's the body. It's sorta crouching down? It really does look like a lion!"

I didn't move a muscle. It was all I could do not to fall back into his arms. But I was barely more than a puddle of water at that point, so I doubted he could hold me.

"You know about Leo the Lion?" Web asked me.

Somehow, I managed to force out the word "No."

"He was this lion from a long time ago. You've heard of Hercules, right?"

"Yeah," I said.

"Well, some god made Hercules go crazy, so he killed his own wife and kids. When Hercules got normal again, he was really sad about what he'd done. So this oracle-lady told him he could make everything okay again if he could do these twelve impossible tasks. The Twelve Labors of Hercules."

"Oh," I said. Web hadn't moved from behind me;

he was still resting his arm on my shoulder and talking into my ear. So now I could smell him too (soap, woodsmoke, and a hint of clean sweat).

"For the first task, Hercules had to kill Leo the Lion," Web said. "But this wasn't just any lion. He was extra strong, and he had this, like, super-hard skin. Hercules tried to shoot arrows at it, but they just bounced off. He tried to kill the lion with his sword, but the metal bent. And he tried to pound it with a club, but the club just broke into a hundred pieces. So you know what Hercules did?"

"No," I said.

"He *strangled* the lion with his bare hands! And when the lion was dead, Hercules took one of Leo's own claws—the only thing sharp enough to cut through the lion's extra-strong skin!—and he skinned it. Then Hercules started wearing the lion's skin himself, and that gave *him* super-hard skin!"

"Wow," I said, and that's when it occurred to me that since Web and I had left to go on our rounds, I had not said a single thing that wasn't a one-word answer.

When I didn't say anything more than my usual single word, Web broke away from me at last. "Well," he said. "We should probably go check on the guys' cabins now."

This was so stupid! Why wasn't I saying anything? Here I was, finally alone with this guy I was so hot for, and I couldn't manage to say anything more than a damn "Wow"?

I needed to say *something*—tell him what a great story that was, ask him what brand of soap he used! *Anything!*

"What about Orion?" I said at last, in a voice just above a whisper. "Where's that in the sky?"

"Huh?" Web said, but not from nearby. He was a good ten feet away from me now. In other words, he'd already moved on across the grass, toward the boys' cabins. I'd finally said something, but he'd been too far away to hear it!

"Russel?" Web said. "You say somethin'?"

"No," I said. Suddenly, I was back in puddle mode.

"Oh," Web said.

And so, with nothing else to say, the two of us walked wordlessly on through the night.

# Chapter Six

**The** next morning, I was still kicking myself for what had—or hadn't!—happened the night before. Web had clearly been flirting with me, hadn't he? So why hadn't I responded—or even *spoken*? It was no wonder he'd lost interest! I felt about as sexy as a plastic reindeer.

More than anything, I was determined never to blow it like that again. Remember that scene in *Gone With the Wind* when Scarlett O'Hara stands with an upraised fist in the desolation that is the Tara plantation after the Civil War, and vows to herself that if she has to lie, cheat, or steal, she'll never go hungry again? That was me when it came to Web: as God was my witness, I was never going to let an opportunity to get cozy with him pass me by again.

I was still thinking about Web that afternoon when I had lifeguard duty with Em.

"So," she said as we sat together on the beach, "who's your Brand?"

"What?" I said. Was she asking me what kind of shoes I liked, or what? That didn't seem like her kind of question at all.

"From that old movie *The Goonies*?" Em said. "Brand is the cool kid. Every cabin has one. Who's yours?"

"Oh," I said, smiling. "Definitely Ian. Ian is *so* Brand. But at least he's human. He keeps losing his flashlight."

"Who's your Data?"

"The brain? Blake, I guess."

"Chunk?"

"The outcast? I hope I don't have one. By the way, I always thought it was so mean that that movie had a fat character named Chunk. What was that about? Spielberg's supposed to be this big humanitarian or whatever."

"Fat bigotry," Em said. "Truly the last acceptable prejudice."

I thought for a second. "I guess the one kid my kids tease the most is Willy. He refuses to take a shower, so he smells."

"Uh-huh," said Em. "Like my kid Caitlin."

"At first, I thought it was the whole group shower thing. So I suggested he take a shower in the evening when no one else was around. No go. I always thought little kids *couldn't* stink. That they didn't have sweat glands or something."

"Oh, God, I wish! Thank God for swimming, though. But even that doesn't get Caitlin really clean. I have to be happy if it just kind of settles the dust."

"Wait," I said. "Little girls stink too?"

"If you don't believe me, come around my cabin sometime. It's like a bad science fiction movie. *The Kid with the Amazing Stink!*"

I laughed. "They're all around us!" Then I started making *woo-woo* science fiction sound effects.

"Oh yeah!" Em said. "Definitely cue the theremin!"

I stopped laughing. "Wait a minute," I said, amazed and astounded. "You know what a theremin is?"

She looked at me. "Of course. Doesn't everybody?"

Okay, this was too weird. As long as I'd known him, Gunnar had been crazy to get a girlfriend. *And* he was crazy for theremins. And now, completely by accident, I had met the one girl on the whole entire planet who actually knew what one was. It was fate. Gunnar and Em were *destined* to be together.

Except that Gunnar had said he'd given up girls. And if I told him about her, I knew what he'd say: Thanks, but no thanks. The last time I'd mentioned Em, he'd shot me down outright.

No, I thought. Em was too perfect. I *had* to get the two of them together. True, Gunnar had *said* he didn't want a girlfriend anymore, but I just knew he wasn't telling the truth. Why else would he be reading romance novels? It was like that theremin he hadn't gotten for Christmas. He could *say* he hadn't wanted it anymore, but anyone who knew him knew it wasn't true. And anyway, hadn't I just made myself a vow never to let a romantic opportunity pass me by again? True, I'd been talking about myself and Web, but the same principle applied here.

"Hey," I said to Em. "You busy tonight?"

She stood up and shouted down to some kids at the edge of the lake, "Knock it off! Let the fish go!" They had caught some minnows in a bucket and were now shooting at them with squirt guns.

She looked back at me, and in typical lifeguard fashion, we picked up our conversation exactly where we'd left off. "Why?" she said. "You asking me out?"

"Uh, no," I said.

"Yeah, I figured I'm not really your type."

I wasn't sure what to say to that. Was she saying what I thought she was saying?

"It's okay," she said. "I'm cool."

"How—?"

"Good gaydar."

"Really?" And I immediately wanted to add, What does your gaydar say about Web?

"No," Em said. "I have a friend who goes to your school. She was telling me about this kid named Russel. From what she said, I figured it was you."

Wow, I thought. I'm famous. For the exact last thing in the world that I wanted to be famous for.

"But don't worry," Em went on. "No one else here knows about you. And I sure won't tell." She looked at me for a second more, then said, "So? What were you going to ask me?"

"Oh," I said, still lost in thought about the whole famous-for-being-gay thing. "Well, there's someone I wanted you to get to know better."

"A guy?"

I nodded.

"Who?" she asked.

"Hmm," I said. "Why don't we make it a surprise?"

"A blind date, huh?" She thought for a second,

then shrugged. "What the hell. It's gonna be a long summer. Where?"

That was a good question. Where could I get Em and Gunnar together where they'd have a little privacy?

Then I saw the perfect place, near the dock. "The boathouse," I said. It was really just this weather-beaten old building where they stored the camp canoes and rowboats. But aren't lovers in books and movies always meeting down at the boathouse?

On my break from lifeguarding, I went to see Gunnar again in the camp store.

"Hey," I said.

"Hey," he said.

On my way over to see him, I'd decided not to tell him outright about my plans. No, I was going to get Gunnar hooked up with a girlfriend without his ever even knowing I was involved.

"Guess what?" I asked. "There's this great big hornets' nest in the boathouse." Gunnar liked bees; I think he was fascinated by how orderly they are. I liked bees too, but not as much as I liked movies like *Gone With the Wind*.

"Really?" Gunnar said.

"Yeah. I'll show you. Meet me in the boathouse right after dinner."

"Cool!" he said, and I thought, Oh, this is too easy. It was just like, well, shooting fish in a bucket.

I left dinner early and went to make sure everything was ready for Gunnar and Em's rendezvous in the boathouse. It had been built on pilings above the lake, near the camp dock. It wasn't much to look at on the outside—pretty ratty and worn. It wasn't much to look at on the inside, either—full of canoes and rowboats, life jackets, buoy ropes, and, unfortunately, big splotches of sparrow droppings (some a little too fresh). But the boathouse was enclosed on only three sides, with two empty boat slips that were open to the water. That meant there was plenty of privacy and a great view of the lake, which had settled into the perfect after-dinner calm. It had been a dry spring, and there were forest fires in some nearby hills (which was not a good thing), but the haze in the air made for an amazing sunset, with the feathery clouds awash in the most incredible shade of orange.

On my way to the boathouse, I had picked some flowers from around the lodge. I'd thought I could set them somewhere in the boathouse to increase the romance factor. I immediately saw the perfect place. I tossed them gently out onto the surface of the lake, and they lay there, slowly swirling in the filtered light.

Perfect! I thought. In a setting like this, even *I'd* be into Em, and I was gay!

Then I noticed a dead seagull in the corner of the boathouse. That didn't fit into the picture I had in my mind of Gunnar taking Em in his arms and bending her backward in a confident, Rhett Butler–like embrace.

But before I could kick the dead bird into the water, I heard wood squeak on the dock outside the boathouse. "Russ?" a voice said. Gunnar.

Shit! I thought. He was early! I had planned to be long gone by the time he and Em arrived. If I was there, I'd ruin everything.

One of the stored rowboats was covered by a canvas, so I slipped inside the boat and crouched down under the cover.

"Russ?" Gunnar said, entering the boathouse. "You here?"

What was I doing, hiding from him like this? But I couldn't tell him I was there; otherwise he wouldn't get together with Em. So for the time being, I decided to stay hidden under that canvas.

I heard more squeaking as Gunnar walked around the boathouse.

"Russ said there was a hive," he said out loud.

"But where?" Gunnar talked to himself? This was something I didn't know about him.

A moment later, I heard more squeaking on the dock outside the boathouse.

"Russ?" Gunnar said.

"No," said a voice. "It's me." Em, of course. She'd entered the boathouse too. (Whatever happened to people being fashionably late?)

"Oh!" Gunnar said. "Hey!"

"What's up?" Em said.

"What? Oh, I'm waiting for someone. He was going to show me a hive."

"Did you find it?"

"No. Just a lot of sparrows' nests."

"Too bad," Em said. "I love bees."

"Really?" Gunnar sounded surprised.

"Oh, yeah."

Right *on*! I said to myself. This was going even better than I'd expected! Better yet, Em hadn't spilled the beans about my setting her up to meet Gunnar.

"Hey, look!" Em said. "Flowers in the water."

"Huh," Gunnar said. "I wonder where they came from."

Em starting laughing.

"What?" Gunnar said.

"I think I know where they came from," Em said.

"Your friend Russel. I think he's trying to set the two of us up."

Oops, I thought. I really should have made Em promise to be more circumspect. But this wasn't necessarily a bad development, romance-wise. If the two of them saw me as some kind of outside manipulator, that might force them closer together. If nothing else, they could share a laugh at my expense.

Unfortunately, Gunnar wasn't laughing. "No," he said. "Russel wouldn't do that. Not after I told him not to."

I admit I felt a tad guilty when Gunnar said this. Just like I felt guilty eavesdropping on them like I was. But what could I do?

"You told him not to set me up with you?" Em said to Gunnar, sounding understandably offended.

"It's not you," Gunnar said. "It's me!"

Sweet Jesus, he was breaking up with her and they'd barely just met!

"Oh," Em said.

"That didn't come out right," Gunnar said. "Look, I've just had bad luck with girls, okay? I told Russel I didn't want to meet *anyone* right now."

"Oh. Well, I should get back to my kids, anyway."

I heard a pause, then some squeaking, like Em was walking for the door. But before she was gone completely, Gunnar said, "No. Wait."

I didn't hear any more squeaking, so Em must have waited.

"What do you like about bees?" Gunnar asked.

"I dunno. They're just cool. You know, it's not true what they say about bumblebees being too heavy for their wings—that their being able to fly violates the laws of aerodynamics. Their wings twist sideways, so there's less drag on the upstroke. That means they follow the laws of aerodynamics just fine."

"Yeah," Gunnar said. "I know."

"I mean, obviously, right? Because they *do* fly."

Hmm, I thought to myself. This was an interesting development. Was Gunnar snatching victory from the jaws of defeat?

The floor to the boathouse squeaked again, like someone was pacing nervously (Gunnar, no doubt).

"You allergic?" he said to Em.

"To bees?" she said. "Yeah. I don't die or anything. I just swell up."

"Me too."

"Careful," Em said. "Don't step on the seagull."

"Huh?" Gunnar said. "Oh!" I heard more squeaks—little ones, like someone was stumbling backward.

Then I heard a squishy sound, followed by a word that struck terror deep into my heart.

*"Whoa!"* was the word, and Gunnar was the one who said it.

Even though I still couldn't see, somehow I knew exactly what was happening out in that boathouse. Gunnar had lurched back from the dead seagull, then slipped on some of the fresh sparrow droppings.

I thought to myself, Please don't let him fall backward into one of the open boat slips!

But even as I thought this, I heard the splash.

"Oh, God!" Em said. "Are you okay?"

Gunnar didn't flail around or anything. Why would he? The water was barely waist-deep in those boat slips. But he had definitely fallen *into* that water. I could hear it lapping against him, and against the pilings underneath the boathouse.

"It's okay," Gunnar said softly. "I'm okay."

"Here," Em said. "Let me help you up."

"No, I'm fine. I'll see you later, okay?"

"What?"

"I'd just kind of like to be alone right now, if you don't mind."

"Oh," Em said. "Are you sure you don't need—?"

"I'm sure."

Em paused a second. "That could've happened to anyone, you know. I could have slipped on that bird shit too."

"Em," Gunnar said evenly. "Please?"

"Okay."

And with that, she left.

After she was gone, poor Gunnar climbed his way back into the boathouse.

Then I heard words that struck terror even deeper into my heart.

"Russ," he said, still speaking oh-so-gently, "I know you're in here."

How had he known? He must have just figured it out, because I was certain he hadn't known I was there when he'd been talking with Em (or to himself).

There was no point in trying to keep up the charade, so I crawled sheepishly out from under that canvas.

"Gunnar," I said, "I am so sorry."

Gunnar didn't say anything, just stared at me. He had the strangest expression on his face—a cross between confusion and pain. Then he pointed his index finger at me and started waggling it. It was like he was so angry, he couldn't even talk to me. He could only shake.

Except he wasn't angry. I saw that now. He was crying. And that just made me feel about a thousand times worse. The thing he had most feared about trying to get a girlfriend—that he would totally embarrass himself in front of her—had come true with a vengeance.

"Oh, Gunnar!" I said. "I am so, *so* sorry! Can you ever forgive me?"

He didn't forgive me. Tears streaming down his cheeks, he turned and ran from the boathouse. He slammed the door in my face, and I didn't blame him in the least.

I had screwed up. I knew it, and Gunnar knew it. Still, I also knew that he'd forgive me eventually. He had to. He'd done something to me a few months earlier that was almost as stupid, and *I'd* forgiven *him*.

Even so, I figured I'd give him a day or so to cool off. I still hadn't talked to Min since we'd had our little spat three days earlier—by now, she *had* had enough time to cool off—so I asked her to meet me down at the secret cove after lights-out. After all, we had plenty to talk about: not just the stuff about Gunnar, but also my encounter with Web the night before, looking up at the stars, and the even *more* interesting encounter with him in the camp showers.

I got to the cove first—I'd put my kids down in almost no time. (Who knew? It turns out I was a master camp counselor after all!)

This time, I didn't climb up on the big granite rock. I waited on the beach. But as I waited, I noticed that the rock did remind me of something after all (and not just the Rock of Gibraltar). It looked like a deflated wedding cake.

A few minutes later, I heard the crunch of footsteps in the dark.

"Min?" I said. She'd been frosty with me for a while now, so I was a little worried that she'd still be miffed.

"Russel!" she said excitedly. "Hey!" She almost skipped out toward me. But that meant she'd forgiven me, right?

"You seem happy," I said to her. "What's up?"

"You'll never believe it!" she said. And then she spoke the horrible words that I knew I would remember until the day I died: "Web and I hooked up!"

# Chapter Seven

**So** Min and Web had gotten together. How was this possible? I knew Min was bi, but I'd never known her to be seriously hot for a guy before. I saw now that this was why she'd been so eager to be his partner those first few days, and why she'd been so insistent a couple of nights before that he wasn't gay (big-time *duh!*). As for Web, the question in my mind had been whether or not he liked *me*, not whether or not he liked guys in general. Talk about putting the conditioner before the shampoo!

"Wow," I said to Min, that night in the cove. "That's great. I'm happy for you."

"Really?" she said. "Because I know you liked him too."

"No. I mean, yeah, I'm a little disappointed. But

hey, if he's straight, he's straight. And if he's straight, well, I'd rather have him hanging out with you than with Lorna." Lorna was one of the other counselors, a real cheerleader-and-headband type.

Min smiled. "Thanks, Russel." Then she happened to glance back toward camp.

"What?" I asked.

"Huh? Oh, nothing."

"Are you meeting Web tonight?"

"No! Well, maybe. But I don't have to leave just yet."

"Go on," I said.

Her face brightened like a halogen lamp. "Really?"

"Yeah."

"Thanks, Russel! You're fantastic!"

And before I could say anything else, she turned and bounded off into the darkness like an eager puppy.

On the way back to my cabin, I ran into Gunnar.

"Hi!" I said. "How you doin'?" What I really meant was, Have you forgiven me yet?

"Hi," he said. "I'm okay." What *he* really meant was, No.

One of my best friends had hooked up with the object of my affections, and my other best friend was so mad that he was barely even talking to me.

I was not having a good week.

That Friday, we took the kids on another all-camp hike. We went south along the water on something called the Waterfront Trail, which mostly followed the shoreline of the lake. There was still a haze in the sky from those distant forest fires, but the real fog was in my mind, from the fact that I felt so at odds with my two best friends and I had no idea what to do about it.

We'd been walking for thirty minutes or so when I came upon Otto on the trail. My kids were overtaking his. For the time being, I was hiking right behind him.

"Hey," I said.

"Oh, hey!" he said, turning to me. Somewhere in the branches overhead, a crow cawed.

For the record, ten-year-old boys don't have a lot of patience or tact, especially when it comes to passing other kids on a trail.

"Hey!" I said to my kids. "No pushing! If you guys want to pass someone, wait your turn."

Sure enough, my kids actually waited their turn.

"Hmm," Otto said. "I guess things are better with your kids, huh?"

"What?" I said.

"When we talked before, you said you were having trouble."

"Oh, yeah." I *had* been having trouble with my kids. But not anymore. Things were so good, I'd almost forgotten about my problems before. "Well, that was good advice you gave. It worked. Thanks."

Up ahead, our kids were stopping and gathering around a ramshackle old cabin by the edge of the lake. It had to have been built and abandoned years ago, and now the roof had mostly fallen in. It looked like a game of Jenga after the blocks had collapsed. In the long grass alongside the cabin, there was the scattered rubble of a fallen stone chimney, and even a bent and rusted metal trough of some sort.

"What is it?" one of Otto's kids asked him.

"Kepler's Homestead," he said. "Built by one of the early lake settlers. It's over a hundred years old."

There was just enough of the front of the cabin left standing that you could step inside for a few yards. So of course, all our kids immediately wanted to go in. They sounded like a bunch of squeaking mice.

"No!" Otto said. "It's not safe. And I don't want anyone getting any ideas about coming back here alone."

"What would you do?" Ian asked.

"Kick your butt. And then call your parents and have them come take you home. Trust me, you'd be in *big* trouble, and your parents would *not* be happy."

"What's *that*?" said one of Otto's kids. He was pointing beyond the cabin, out across the lake.

We all looked.

There was gray smoke billowing up from behind the wooded hills on the opposite side of the water. It was the kind of smoke that could only be coming from a forest fire.

I had known there were fires burning somewhere—I'd seen the haze in the air for days now. But I hadn't known they were so close to camp. I'm not sure what was different here—the angle from the Waterfront Trail or the fact that the lake was so much narrower here, barely a quarter mile across.

But even with the new view, it was impossible to know exactly how close that fire was, or even how big it was. It could have been burning right on the other side of that hill, or maybe it was miles and miles away and the smoke just made it *look* close. And it could have been the smoke of an isolated little fire already burning itself out—or maybe it was the result of some great conflagration burning out of control.

"It's nothing," Otto said at last. "Let's keep going."

"It's *not* nothing!" Ian said. "It's a fire!"

"Way on the other side of the lake," I said. "We're perfectly safe here. And look, the firefighters are already putting it out." Sure enough, there were helicopters approaching, no doubt preparing to dump water on the blaze. Why hadn't I noticed the copters before? I guess I had, but I'd assumed they were tourists out sightseeing.

"But what about the trees that are already on fire?" one of Otto's kids asked. "Won't they die?"

"Not the grown ones," Otto said. "Their bark is special. When trees get really old, their bark develops these fire-retardant properties. It protects them from fires."

"It does not!" Kwame said.

"Yeah, it does."

"But they'll still be hurt, won't they?" one of Otto's kids said.

"No," Otto said. "They'll survive."

"But they'll still feel pain!" another kid said.

"No," Otto said. "They're trees. Trees don't feel pain."

"They do so!" Ian said.

"No!" Otto said, losing his composure at last. "They *don't*!"

I may not be the smartest guy in the world, but

even I could tell that Otto and the kids weren't just talking about trees. They were burn survivors, and in some strange way, Otto and those kids were really talking about themselves.

I looked at them, staring out across the lake in silence. Every single one of them was transfixed, like he was seeing a ghost, which I guess they kind of were. One way or another, they'd all seen that fire up close (well, except for Julian with his acne conglobata—but he was watching that fire pretty intently too).

I looked at Otto. Now even he was being hypnotized by the smoke. I was the only one not spellbound by the sight. So I figured I should say something. But what? Part of me didn't want to intrude on their moment, except it didn't seem like a good moment. It felt like they were scared, stuck in place, unable to move forward. But it also didn't seem right just to say, *Okay, guys, time to push on!* like I was pretending what was happening wasn't happening at all.

In the trees overhead, the crow cawed again.

And suddenly, I had an idea.

"The Lenape Indians have a legend about fire," I said to the whole group. Otto glanced at me, curious as to what I was up to, but the kids were all still staring across the lake.

"It all started back when there were just animals on the Earth," I went on. "Before humans—before seasons, even—back when the weather was always warm. But then, one day, winter came, and snow fell for the very first time. At first, the animals liked it, but as it continued to fall they began to get cold. So they met together to figure out what to do. And in the end, they decided to send one of the animals to the distant home of the Creator, to ask him to stop the snow."

I looked around. The kids were still staring across the lake, but they seemed to be listening to me too (well, except for Ian, who was now busy kicking the stones from the collapsed fireplace).

I had to think hard to remember the rest of the story. I was pretty sure it was even better than the one Web had told me about Hercules and Leo the Lion.

"The animals were going to send Owl to see the Creator," I said, "but they worried that he'd get confused in the daylight. And they couldn't send Coyote, because they figured she'd get distracted. So they decided to send the most beautiful of all the animals, Rainbow Crow. Because back then, the crow had feathers with all the colors of the rainbow, and a singing voice that was the most beautiful of all the birds'.

"Rainbow Crow agreed to go see the Creator, and flew high up into the sky, above the snow and wind and clouds and moon and stars. He flew for three days, and finally he reached his destination. But the Creator was too busy to see the crow. So Rainbow Crow started singing, and the sound was so beautiful that the Creator stopped what he was doing and came to Rainbow Crow and said, 'By singing that song, you have given me a great gift. Now I want to give you a gift. What shall I give you?'

"Rainbow Crow said, 'Please, Sir, it is so cold down on Earth. I would like you to stop the snow.'

"The Creator said to the crow, 'I'm sorry, I can't do that, because the snow has a spirit of its own, as do the wind and the winter. But I can give you a gift to use against the cold. I can give you the gift of fire, and that will keep you and the other animals warm.'

"So," I continued with my story, "the Creator picked up a stick and put it into the sun, setting it on fire. Then he gave it to Rainbow Crow, saying, 'Unfortunately, I can only give you this gift one time, so hurry back to Earth before the flame goes out.'"

As I was talking, I looked around at the kids again. They weren't just listening: now they were hanging on my every word—even Ian, who had stopped kicking the stones. I knew that it wasn't because I was such a great storyteller. No, it was because they were scared and they wanted something from me and my story, even if I still wasn't quite sure what that was.

"So Rainbow Crow took the Creator's flaming stick in his beak," I said, "and started flying the three-day journey home. But as he flew, ashes from the fire blew back into his feathers, turning them black with soot. And as the fire burned, the smoke blew into his mouth, and his voice became cracked and hoarse.

"Eventually, Rainbow Crow made it back to Earth, and he shared the fire with the other animals. With it, they melted the snow and became warm and happy. But Rainbow Crow was sad, because by now his fantastic rainbow-colored feathers had turned black and his beautiful singing voice was gone. He wasn't Rainbow Crow anymore. Now he was just Crow. So he flew to the top of a tree where he could be alone and cry.

"Now, up in the heavens, the Creator heard Crow crying and felt his great despair, and so he came down to the bird. 'Why are you so sad?' the Creator asked.

" 'I'm sad,' Crow said, 'because I was once beautiful, but I'm not anymore. I once had a great singing voice, but now I don't. I am no longer Rainbow Crow, but just Crow.'

" 'What you did for your people took great

courage,' the Creator said. 'And as a reward, I have given you those blackened feathers, and a different kind of singing voice. They are my gift to you—the gift of freedom.'

"'*Freedom?*' Crow said. 'How are these things the gift of freedom?'

"'You have saved your people from the cold,' the Creator said. 'But soon there will be a new threat facing the animals. Soon humans will come to Earth, and they will take your fire and try to be master of everything. But they will never master you. Humans won't hunt you for food or feathers, because now your meat tastes of smoke and your feathers are black. And they won't capture and cage you, because now your voice is coarse. You will always be Rainbow Crow, and you will still be beautiful, but it will be a secret beauty, one that others will not see unless they look very carefully.' And sure enough, when Crow looked down at his black feathers, he saw that, in a certain light, they still shone with all the colors of the rainbow.

"And so Crow returned to the other animals. And to this day, only a very few humans can see the secret beauty of the freest of all the animals, Rainbow Crow."

When I finished, I looked around at the kids again. Those distant helicopters still sputtered and the lake still gurgled, but the kids themselves were absolutely quiet.

It was funny. When I'd started the story, I'd just been thinking it was a nice, distracting little story about fire. But now that I'd finished, I saw that it was the perfect story for these burn survivor kids, about how they were all Rainbow Crows too, with hidden beauty. For a second, I thought of saying something about this. But I didn't know how to express it without sounding stupid. So instead, I said, very quietly, "Let's get moving, okay?"

Still without a word, we started down the trail again. And then—and this couldn't have gone better if I'd planned it!—the crow began to caw. Every kid stared up at that bird, no longer hypnotized by the distant forest fire but by the crow, and by my story.

Finally, Otto said to me, "Is that a real Indian legend?"

"I think so," I said.

"Where did you hear it?"

"In this novel about the American frontier. It really stuck with me."

"It's beautiful." Was it my imagination, or was Otto a little choked up? I looked over at him, but I was seeing the scarred side of his face, so I couldn't tell what his expression was, what he was thinking.

"I liked your music," I said. "The other night around the campfire? That was beautiful too."

"Oh," Otto said, and he looked down at the ground. "Thanks."

Now I did know what he was thinking, because scarred face or not, Otto Digmore was blushing.

## Chapter Eight

I am not one to blow my own horn, but let's get one thing straight here and now: as a camp counselor for burn survivors, I rocked.

No, I didn't just rock. By telling that story about Rainbow Crow when the kids had been so freaked by that forest fire, I had proven once and for all that I was the mighty God of Camp Counselors, sipping from a golden Camp Counselor Goblet and dwelling on the top of Mount Camp Counselor Olympus!

Let's just say I felt pretty damn good about myself. And I was thinking about all this that night after lights-out as I made my way back to my cabin after hanging out down at the campfire with the other counselors.

Almost home, I heard the sound of laughter.

Web's laughter.

I also heard the sound of splashing, and it was coming from the direction of that secluded little cove with the rock, the place where I'd been meeting Min and Gunnar at night. So another counselor—Web—had found our secret cove at last. He hadn't been down at the campfire with the rest of us, and I couldn't help but wonder what he had to be laughing about. Except Min hadn't been at the campfire either, so I already had a pretty good idea.

Sure enough, a second later, I heard more laughing—a girl's laughter.

Min's laughter.

Whatever was happening between the two of them, I suddenly had to see it for myself. I turned and started down the trail toward the secret cove. At the same time—and this is where things start to get a little dubious—I took that trail slowly, being careful not to step on any branches or twigs, basically trying not to make any noise. I wasn't sneaking up on Web and Min exactly, but let's just say I didn't necessarily want to announce my presence to the world.

As I neared the beach, I turned onto a different trail, one that led up to a little rocky ledge that looked down into the cove from one side. That way, I'd be able to see into the cove, but Web and Min wouldn't be able to see me.

Out on the ledge, I worked my way through the undergrowth until I had a clear view of the water below. The first thing I noticed was the big granite rock—that it looked different from this angle. It didn't look like a wedding cake or the Rock of Gibraltar (whatever *that* looked like). From where I was, it looked like a sinking ship.

There were two people in the water below that rock, swimming and talking and laughing. Sure enough, one of them was Web. And the other was Min. It was dark and I couldn't see anything clearly, but somehow I just knew that they were skinny-dipping.

Web hadn't "found" our secret little cove—Min had *shown* it to him! The nerve!

Anyway, I'd seen what I'd come to see, so I'd like to be able to say I turned around and went back to my cabin.

I'd like to be able to say that, but I can't, because that's not what happened.

No, what happened was that I crouched down into the undergrowth and watched the two of them frolic in the moonlit water. I know this makes me sound like some pervert voyeur (especially after I eavesdropped on Gunnar and Em in the boathouse!). And I am also completely aware that this was a total invasion of their privacy or whatever. But somehow I just couldn't help myself.

As I crouched there in the bushes, Web suddenly swam toward the big rock and climbed up onto it. It was almost as if I was controlling him with my mind, because this is just what I would have commanded him to do.

As he stood up tall on that rock, I saw I had been right. They were skinny-dipping. Web was completely naked. And he was standing right in the moonlight, so I could see everything.

I had seen Web naked before—that night in the shower house. But that had just been a quick look while his head was covered. This was different. Now I could stare. He didn't know I was there. It was completely wrong of me, I knew that, and I knew I'd probably have to pay for it after I died, in purgatory or whatever (if such a place really exists).

But I didn't care. Because it was worth it. Standing there glistening in the light of the silver moon, Web was beautiful.

My dad collects books of *Peanuts* comic strips— the ones with Charlie Brown and Lucy and Snoopy? And my watching Web like that reminded me of one series of those *Peanuts* strips. In the comic, Peppermint Patty, who is in love with Charlie

Brown, sees the Little Red-Haired Girl, the girl Charlie Brown is in love with, for the very first time. Peppermint Patty wants to talk to her, but the only thing she can do is cry. She sees just how beautiful the Little Red-Haired Girl is, and why Charlie Brown is so in love with her. "She just sort of sparkles," Peppermint Patty says. And Peppermint Patty realizes that she'll never be that beautiful, and that no one will ever look at her the way Charlie Brown looks at the Little Red-Haired Girl.

Standing on that rock, Web was sparkling too, and not just because of the water and the moonlight. His body was perfect, and I wanted to cry because I knew I would never look like that, and that no one could ever look at me the way I was looking at him.

Only with me, it was more than that. I wanted to cry not just because Web was so beautiful. It was also because I now knew he was straight and he'd chosen Min for a girlfriend, and I would never know that beauty, and probably wouldn't even be able to ever look at it again. (Who knows? Maybe Peppermint Patty was crying over the Little Red-Haired Girl for exactly the same reason. She always did strike me as a baby dyke.)

And before I could stop myself, I really did choke up a bit. Because of the acoustics of the bay and the fact that the night was so still, my little cough echoed down into the cove.

Web looked up toward the ledge. "Hello?" he said. "Is someone there?"

I froze. It was one of those situations where I just could *not* be caught, because there was nothing short of the truth that could explain why I was where I was. And the truth was just so beyond embarrassing.

"It's nothing," Min called. "Come on—jump!"

He did. And with the splash of the water, I was able to creep from that ledge to the trail, where I could then carefully make my way back to my cabin.

I can honestly say I felt horribly guilty about spying on them and violating their privacy like that. Unfortunately, if I'm going to be *completely* honest, I also have to admit that if I had that evening to live one more time, I would do the exact same thing all over again.


The next day, Saturday, the whole camp went on a field trip to a nearby logging camp. More specifically, an old logging camp that had since been turned into an open-air museum.

If I were to describe the whole field trip, you'd be as bored as the kids (pretty darn bored). So I'll try and stick to the non-boring parts, which, rest assured, have nothing whatsoever to do with logging.

The first interesting thing happened on the bus on the way there. Em sat next to me, and at one point she leaned close to me and said, "I like him."

I sat back from her a little, mostly because I was worried about my breath. "What?" I said.

"Your friend Gunnar. He's cute."

I could only stare. "Are you kidding?"

She laughed. "Why would I be kidding?"

I glanced at the kids and counselors sitting around us. Gunnar was on the other bus, but I couldn't be sure someone wouldn't overhear us and tell him what we'd been talking about. Bad breath or not, I leaned in toward Em. "What about what happened at the boathouse?" I whispered. I didn't want her knowing I'd eavesdropped on them, so I added, "Gunnar told me what happened."

She shrugged. "It wasn't anything."

"What about how he fell in?"

"He just slipped. It could've happened to anyone."

"You really believe that?"

She was looking at me like I was bonkers. "Uh, yeah."

Em liked Gunnar. How was this possible? For her to like him after he'd made such a fool of himself, she had to be in violation of at least several laws of physics.

Em twiddled with her hair. "Does he like me?"

"I don't know," I said. "It never really came up."

"Do you think maybe you could . . . ?"

"What?"

"You know. Get us together again?"

Em wanted me to set her up with Gunnar again? This was incredible! All his life, he'd wanted a girlfriend, and now one was falling right into his lap! And a great girlfriend, no less.

"Wait," I said, remembering. There was no way Gunnar would let me set him up with her again. He'd been absolutely clear about that. "No," I said.

"No what?"

"Em, Gunnar's barely even talking to me now. Because of the first time I tried to set you guys up."

"Well, when he does talk to you again, would you tell him I like him? I'd do it myself, but I think he's avoiding me."

"He *is* avoiding you. He's avoiding all girls. He thinks he's cursed or something."

"Come on, Russel. I really like the guy!"

"But—"

"Will you at least talk to him? How could that possibly hurt?"

I thought about this. She had a point. It couldn't hurt to at least *talk* to him.

I didn't have to wait long for a chance to have that chat. It happened at the logging camp. It was the second interesting thing that happened on that field trip.

I was watching my kids as they climbed around on one of the abandoned locomotives on the museum grounds.

Gunnar sidled up next to me. "Your kids have been great today," he said.

"Oh!" I said. "Thanks!" It was the first real sentence he'd spoken to me since the incident in the boathouse.

"For the record, I'm done being mad at you."

"Really? That's great. Thanks! Thanks for forgiving me."

We didn't say anything for a second. Then he said, "So what's going on?"

"Oh. Nothing much."

"What?" Gunnar said. "You look like you want to say something."

I *did* want to say something (the thing about Em), but I hated the fact that my face was so easy to read. Did that mean Web could see my feelings so clearly?

"Yeah?" I said casually. "No. It's nothing."

"Russ."

"Oh, God. Okay. But don't talk for a second, okay? Just listen." I turned to face him. "I rode here on the bus with Em. She told me she still likes you. She even asked me to set you guys up again."

I stared at him. He didn't say anything.

"Okay," I said. "You can talk now."

"You're kidding," he said. "Right?"

"No! She just told me."

"Not about that. About the fact that you're still trying to set me up with a girl! And not even thirty seconds after I decide to start talking to you again! Have you even been listening to the things I've been telling you?"

"No, I've been listening. But this is different, because—"

"Russ? I know you mean well. But stop it. It's over. I don't want a girlfriend. Not Em, not anyone. Okay?"

What could I do? I looked at him and nodded.

"Do you promise?"

"What?"

"I want you to promise me you won't try to hook me up with Em or any other girl."

I sighed and nodded. "Okay."

"Say it," he said. "Say it out loud."

"Gunnar!" Now he was rubbing it in.

But just as I'd done with Ian in that patch of poison oak, Gunnar kept glaring at me until I finally said my promise out loud. And I wasn't even crossing my fingers at the time.

The last thing that happened on that field trip was the most interesting of all. Unfortunately, it's also pretty embarrassing to me. But it's kind of important to the story, so I have to include it anyway.

My kids wanted to go into the gift shop. This was a bad idea for a lot of reasons, like the fact that they'd probably buy lots of candy to make themselves even more hyperactive, and that the store would probably be full of delicate glass trinkets for them to knock over and break. But after my Rainbow Crow story, I felt like I was on a Camp Counselor Roll, and I was convinced I could handle my kids under almost any circumstances.

Sure enough, there were lots of fragile things in that gift shop—plates and porcelain collectibles and crystal figurines. There were also four other people—two guys and two girls, all teenagers. I noticed them immediately (all right, I noticed the *guys* immediately because, well, they were both totally hot). They were older than me, probably seniors. And they were the worst kind of cute—trim and cocky and rich, with their flashy board shorts and Versace sunglasses. In fact, they looked like the kind of totally cool jock guys who had given me so much grief back at my school. (The bane of almost every gay boy's existence: sometimes the biggest high school jerks are also the hunkiest.)

I tried my best to ignore those teenage guys. They had no way of knowing I was gay—not as long as I kept myself from drooling (difficult, but doable). So they had no reason to bother me. Since they were obviously straight, they probably wouldn't even notice I was there.

Then I remembered that I hadn't come into that gift shop alone. I had come in with my kids.

My burned and scarred and disfigured kids.

By this point in the camp session, I'd mostly forgotten that my kids even had scars. But suddenly, I saw my kids through the eyes of those two hunky-but-probably-jerky senior dudes. It wasn't hard to imagine what they'd think of Zach (Phantom of the Opera, here we come!).

Sure enough, they immediately looked over at my kids.

No, they didn't just look. They *stared*. The girl-friends were being a little more circumspect, but they were basically staring too.

Suddenly, I had a very bad feeling about this.

My kids noticed the stares. There hadn't been anyone else out in the logging camp open-air museum, so this was the first time any of them had been stared at since the start of camp a week before.

I immediately felt embarrassed. I wasn't sure what for. My kids sure didn't have anything to be embarrassed about for being burn survivors. And I didn't have anything to be embarrassed about by being their camp counselor. But I *was* embarrassed. And the best way I can explain it is by saying that being with them suddenly felt very, very familiar. It felt exactly the way I had felt walking down the halls of Robert L. Goodkind High School every day as The Gay Kid. I didn't have anything to be embarrassed for about that either, but I sure had been.

More than anything in the world, I wanted out of that gift shop, away from those teenage boys and (to be totally honest) away from my kids. I was tired of being the freak, the center of attention. That was the reason why I'd come to be a counselor at Camp Serenity in the first place.

"Come on," I said to my kids. "Let's head back to the others." None of my kids said a word. I think they were all feeling variations on the discomfort I was experiencing and wanted to leave too. So we all started walking for the door.

And everything would have been just fine, no one ever would have known about my secret embarrassment or anything, if at that exact moment one of those teenage boys hadn't said, perfectly loudly, "Fuckin' freaks!" Then the other guy—but neither of the girls—laughed.

When my kids heard this—and they *did* all hear it, because it was the kind of thing they were listening for—they froze. I froze too, but not like a gunslinger who's just heard some desperado curse his mother and is about to whirl on him, guns drawn. No, I froze like a computer screen, feeling frustrated and worthless.

I wanted to turn on those guys and tell them to go fuck themselves. It was the right thing to do. It was definitely what they *deserved*.

But for some reason, I couldn't do it. I was still frozen, in need of a complete reboot. And as everyone with a computer knows, a reboot takes a very long time—more time than I had to recover my senses.

So I just stood there. Why didn't I speak up? Why did I care that they might turn their sights on me? I'd never *see* them again! All I can say is that I was frozen, which even I can see is just about the lamest excuse imaginable. (Man, does this whole day make me look like a jerk or what?)

Anyway, time strung out like a loose thread. But still I didn't say anything to those guys. Even now, my kids were looking to me, their big defender. I was the mother bear to their cubs, and we'd been attacked by hunters.

Finally, I found my voice, except I didn't really. All I said was, "Come on. Let's get out of here." I was talking only to my kids, not to the ones who deserved to be spoken to.

My kids and I kept walking toward the door. You've heard the expression "a bull in a china shop"? That's what I felt like. I even imagined I heard glass breaking all around me. Except it wasn't me or anyone else knocking over all the gift shop's delicate glass trinkets. No, it was my kids' opinions of me, each one falling to the ground and shattering into a thousand unsalvageable pieces.

## Chapter Nine

**Okay**, so maybe I wasn't the mighty Camp Counselor God residing in the Camp Counselor Heavens after all. I had really screwed up in that gift shop. Once outside in the parking lot, I tried to patch things up with my kids by saying, "Just ignore them. Don't let them bother you." But it was way too little, too late. I had spent the whole week trying to convince my kids that it wasn't "me" versus "them" but that we were all just one big "us." But in that one frozen, tongue-tied moment in the gift shop, I had taken us right back to Square One. Except I was now even farther back than Square One, because once someone trusts you and you betray that trust, it's much harder for you to win it back.

By the end of that day, I knew for a fact I was on

Square Negative One. Suddenly, I was on the receiving end of squirt guns again. When we went to the lodge for dinner, our table mysteriously had no place for me to sit. And that night before bed, I had to ask the kids fifteen times to go brush their teeth, not the usual six. I'm not even sure they were completely aware of what they were doing. All I knew was that they had once thought of me as one of them, but they didn't anymore.

I considered reminding them of the promise they'd made several days ago, that afternoon in the patch of poison oak—that they'd listen to me and do what I said until the end of the session. But I didn't say anything. Let's face it: by acting like I had in that gift shop, I had pretty much absolved them of their promise.

I was hoping against hope that it was just a temporary setback—that the kids would forget what had happened and things would go back to normal the following day.

The next morning, I woke up to find my shoes filled with sand.

To make matters worse, it was Parent Visitation Day, which brought a whole bunch of new weirdness.

I would have thought that the kids would be happy to see their parents, and most *were* happy to see their own parents. But along with their own parents came the parents of all the other kids, and their brothers and sisters too.

Non-scarred parents, and non-scarred brothers and sisters.

Most of the kids lived too far away for their families to visit them halfway through the session. But some came, and the end result was that, for the first time since the session had begun, there were more non-scarred people at Camp Serenity than there were scarred people.

In other words, it was *Invasion of the Normal People*!

It wasn't just my kids who were made weird by this. I could sense it in all the kids. They were anxious, jumpy, like cats before an earthquake.

Three of my campers had families visiting. But the only interesting one was Trevor's.

Man, they were good-looking: the mom, the dad, the older brother (*especially* the older brother—yeow!). With their perfect hair and rosy cheeks, they looked even better than a TV family; they looked like a TV-*commercial* family.

I introduced myself to them out on the grass above the beach, and Trevor's mom said to me, "I just want to say how great it is, the work you're doing here." I couldn't help but think she seemed a little nervous being around so many burn survivors, which I understood, but which I also thought was strange, given that her son was one.

."Oh," I said to her. "Well, thanks."

Trevor's dad gave me a sober stare. "So how's he been acting?" he asked me.

"Trevor?" I said. "Oh, he's been great." This was true. Even after the disaster in the gift shop, Trevor was still talking to me and everything.

Trevor's dad kept looking at me. "He hasn't been out of line?"

"No," I said, a little confused. "He's been terrific."

As his parents and I talked, I glanced over at Trevor, who was nearby, tossing horseshoes (where in the hell had the older brother gone?). But that's when I noticed for the first time that Trevor must have been good-looking too, before his accident. Not that he wasn't *still* good-looking. He was. But, well, you know.

After a while, Trevor's mom called him over. "Trevor?" she said. "Let's go get some lunch!"

He didn't react. And he definitely didn't stop playing horseshoes. I thought this was odd. It was almost like he was ignoring them, and that wasn't like him at all. Or had he not heard her?

"Trevor!" his dad yelled. "Get over here *now*!"

Trevor threw his last horseshoe, then finally joined us. Was he scowling? Maybe I was imagining things, or maybe it was the harsh way his dad had yelled at him. I hadn't even known Trevor *could* scowl.

After he and his family went off for lunch together, I had some time to myself (finally!). I went down to the dock to stare out at the water.

I was still thinking about Trevor and his parents. He had almost seemed like a different kid around them. Did it have something to do with the fact they were good-looking and he wasn't—at least not like he had been? If his parents were embarrassed by their son's scars, it made sense that Trevor might resent them, and that he might take it out on them by being a more difficult kid.

"Well?" Em said, suddenly joining me on the dock. "Did you talk to Gunnar?"

"Huh?" It took me a second to remember what she was talking about (I'd had a lot else on my mind). "Oh, yeah," I said. "Sorry, no. It's not that he doesn't like you. He's just too embarrassed. He thinks he's going to make a fool out of himself again."

"Really?"

"Really," I said, thinking, Great, yet another person who's disappointed in me.

It took me forever to get the kids to sleep that night. I knew they were still punishing me for the gift shop incident, and I guess I thought I deserved it, because I put up with it.

When they were finally asleep, I left to join the other counselors down around the campfire, even though I wasn't sure there was anyone down there who particularly wanted to see me.

"Hey," said a voice from the darkness.

"Huh?" I said.

It was Web, leaning against a tree right outside my cabin. It was almost like he'd been waiting for me.

"Headin' down to the beach?" he asked.

"Yeah. I guess."

"Wanna go for a walk?"

"A walk? Where?"

"Dunno. Just a walk."

Web was asking me to go for a walk? I immediately thought of my Scarlett O'Hara–like vow never to blow an opportunity with Web again. But then I remembered Min, and the fact that she was with Web now, and that he was straight anyway.

Still, I thought, it wouldn't kill me to go for a walk with the guy.

"Sure," I said. "Let's walk."

We started down the trail away from camp. And that was when it finally sunk in what was happening.

*I was going on a walk with Web!*

A friendly walk, true. But still a walk.

"So," he said. "How's it goin'? With your kids."

"Oh, it's okay," I said. "Well, no, it's not. It was a bad day. I screwed up, and they're kind of punishing me."

"Yeah?"

"Yeah, we were in the gift shop at that logging camp yesterday, and some older guys were there."

"Hey!" he said suddenly. "Let's go swimming!"

"Swimming?"

"Yeah! I know the perfect place!" And he started almost running down the trail.

Of course, I followed. And in a minute or two, we arrived on the beach at that no-longer-secret cove just north of camp. Sure enough, the big granite rock looked different than it had before. Tonight, it somehow reminded me of a volcano.

"Isn't this great?" he said. "Let's get in!"

"But I didn't bring a suit," I said. I have no idea why I said this. Obviously, he wanted to go skinny-dipping. For some reason, whenever I get into situations like this, my brain goes completely numb.

" 'Sokay," Web said, peeling off his T-shirt. "You

don't tell, I won't tell!" Then he kicked off his sandals, dropped his shorts (he wasn't wearing underwear), and climbed up onto the rock. "Come on!"

Once again, he was completely naked up on that rock, and a lot closer than before (I guess I'd been wrong about never seeing him naked again). But unlike the time before, I didn't dare look. So I stared down at the sand and started taking off my own clothes.

What was going on here? I thought to myself. Were we just two guys out on a friendly walk and now going for an innocent after-hours swim? Or was it something more?

I looked up just in time to see him make a perfect dive from that rock into the water.

When he surfaced, he looked back at me and called, "Come on! Get in!"

I was standing there in just my underwear. Please imagine me looking as studly as humanly possible. The truth is, I looked like a white broomstick with goose bumps. (Someday I *will* fill out!)

"Oh, man!" Web said, splashing around. "This feels great!"

I slipped off my underwear but didn't climb up on the rock, because I didn't want Web to see me (let's just say I was cold and leave it at that, okay?).

Out in the lake, Web did a surface dive, and I took

the opportunity to slide into the water. I'd expected it to be cold, but it wasn't. It felt warm. I'd never swum naked before, and it felt strange—good-strange, not weird-strange. It was like I was being touched all over, even in places where I was definitely not used to being touched.

In fact, it felt a little too good. Those places where I wasn't used to being touched? Suddenly, I had the opposite problem from the one I'd had back on the beach.

Web surfaced not five feet from where I was floating. I started in surprise.

"Whaddaya think?" he said, his face shimmering.

"Huh?" I said. "Oh, it's good. It feels really good."

Suddenly, he submerged again. He'd been facing me when he went under, so there was only one direction for him to go.

"Wait!" I said.

And then I felt him down below, brushing against me. At least I thought it was him. It could have been some kind of lake creature, which I wouldn't necessarily have objected to, because then it would have been the creature, and not Web, that had felt me *there*.

Web surfaced again, behind me now. "Hmmmmmm!" he said. "I'd *say* you think the water feels good, huh?"

Okay, I thought. This was no innocent after-hours swim. Web was hitting on me!

I'd waited my whole life for this moment. I wasn't going to screw it up, not again.

I paddled around to face him. "Sure does," I said. "How does the water make *you* feel?"

He grinned, and the moon glistened in his eyes. "Pretty good. Pretty damn good."

Was this really happening? Was I really doing the whole skinny-dipping/weird flirtatious thing with Web Bastian?

"It almost feels like there's someone touching me," I said. "Down there."

He floated closer. "I feel that too, man."

"Do you?"

"Yeahhh," he whispered. "And it feels *soooo* good." He was less than two feet from me now. The water was lapping at my neck, and I could feel his breath on my face, even wetter than the lake.

He floated closer still—a foot away. We were almost bumping chests.

And that's when I finally remembered something I had momentarily forgotten: whether Web was gay or not, he was now the boyfriend of my best friend!

"Wait!" I said suddenly. "What about Min?"

Web ignored me, just leaned forward and kissed me on the lips.

# Chapter Ten

So Web was kissing me, and it's not like I could not kiss him back. That would have been rude. Yes, he was seeing my best friend, so on one level this wasn't right. But I'd made myself a vow that I wouldn't let an opportunity like this pass me by. Remember? Scarlett O'Hara? Raised fist? And this was the Fort Knox of golden opportunities. So breaking that kiss wouldn't have been right either—right?

I was tingling all over. I could feel every single nerve ending in my entire body, and each one was on red alert (some more alerted than others!).

We were still kissing when I felt his arms slip around me, exploring, but also drawing me close, sucking me in. I'd been seduced by a merman or an octopus, and Min or no Min, I was powerless to escape.

Suddenly, my body was pressing against his, slick and warm and hard, and that's when I *really* knew we were skinny-dipping. There was absolutely nothing coming between Web and me now.

And then he ducked under the water again. Only this time, he did more than brush me with his hand.

Later, the guilt set in. It wasn't that I had done anything unsafe, because I hadn't (and wouldn't!). Maybe it was a little bit about the fact that I'd done what I'd done with a guy I barely knew. I wasn't the kind of person who did stuff like that, was I?

But mostly it was Min. It was that I'd done what I'd done with a guy who was the boyfriend of one of my best friends. And as much as I'd pretended at the time that I'd been powerless, I wasn't really.

"What is it?" Web asked as he lolled in the shallow water where the lake met the beach.

I was sitting upright in the water. It wasn't cold exactly, but I shivered anyway.

I looked over at him. "Min."

"What about her?"

"Well, aren't you with her?"

"Who told you that?"

"She did!"

Web shook his head and leaned back in the water,

his *thing* floating up between his legs. "Nah. We're just friends."

"What?"

"It's true," he said. "What makes you think we're together?"

"Because I saw you—!" I started to say. Then I realized, Oops! I couldn't tell him that I had seen them skinny-dipping, because then I would have to admit that I'd been spying.

"Saw me what?" Web said. I could see the smirk on his lips, even in the dark.

"Together," I finished. "I saw you together."

"Well, sure. Can't friends spend time together?"

Could what he was saying be true? They *could* have gone skinny-dipping as friends, especially if Web was gay. But if Min knew he was gay, why hadn't she told me?

"So you're gay?" I asked.

Web floated in the gentle ripples, splayed out like a cologne model in some glossy magazine. "That was hot," he said, eyes lasering into me. "You think that was hot?"

"I guess," I said, sinking deeper into the water and doing my best to avoid his gaze.

Web sat upright. "Come here."

"What? No, I don't think—"

But then the octopus of Lake Serenity was on the move again. And once again, I was powerless to escape.

The next day, Monday, we started a new counselor rotation. This time, in the morning I had archery duty with Min. Fortunately, we had an adult instructor, so Min and I didn't have to do much except make sure the kids didn't nock their bows the wrong way, or shoot each other.

When I first saw Min, I said, really excitedly, "Hey!" I know Web had told me that he and Min weren't together, but I didn't entirely believe it. Plus when we'd fooled around, Web hadn't yet told me about him and Min not being boyfriend and girlfriend. So technically, I'd betrayed one of my best friends whether they were together or not. Anyway, I felt guilty around Min, which is why I was acting so enthusiastic about seeing her now.

"Oh, hi," she said. She didn't sound particularly enthusiastic about seeing me, which I guess made sense since she didn't have anything to feel guilty about.

I wanted to tell her what had happened with Web. After all, if they were just friends like he'd said, what difference would it make? But instead, I said, "How'd it go on Parent Visitation Day?"

"Not bad," she said. "I think it was a little weird for my kids to be reminded of their other lives. I kind of think most of them want to forget about that."

"Yeah?" I said. "I thought the exact same thing."

"Speaking of which, Mimi's mom brought her a Game Boy. The sound is driving me crazy!"

We went on like that, with both of us talking about whatever had been going on in each of our lives. Everything, that is, except Web Bastian.

Then there were my kids. They still hadn't forgiven me for the gift shop incident. Which meant that unless I figured out some way to reconnect with them, I'd be picking burrs out of my underwear until the end of the session.

That afternoon, in my free time before dinner, I looked around for Web but never did find him. As I searched, I tried to think of some way to get back into my kids' good graces.

I was walking from the lodge to my cabin when I suddenly had the perfect answer.

It was almost eleven o'clock when I woke my kids up from their sleep.

"Huh?" Blake said, confused. "What's happening?"

"Shhh," I said. "Don't talk. Everything's fine. Everyone just get dressed. And don't forget your flashlights."

If this had been a group of adults, or even a group of teenagers, they would have complained that I'd woken them up in the middle of the night. But not one of my kids complained, and I knew it was because there is nothing like doing something out of the ordinary to get the attention of a ten-year-old boy.

Once they were dressed, I led them out into the summer night.

"Where are we going?" Julian said, still a little groggy.

"You'll see," I said. "Just follow me. But be very quiet. Keep your flashlights turned off until we're away from the camp grounds. And if we run into any other counselors, we may have to lie low for a second, okay?"

For the record, I'd told the other counselors that I had something planned and not to worry if anyone found us missing in the middle of the night. But I knew my kids would be more excited if they thought we were doing something *against the rules* (for a ten-year-old boy, the only thing better than something out of the ordinary is when that something is also against the rules). And it was working. None of my kids were groggy now.

We walked silently across the camp grounds to the trailhead of the Waterfront Trail. It led south toward Kepler's Homestead, the abandoned cabin where we'd witnessed the smoke of that forest fire across the lake.

Otto was waiting for us at the trailhead.

"It's okay," I said to my kids. "He's with us."

For safety reasons, I'd needed another counselor to help with what I had in mind. So I'd asked Otto and told him to meet us here. But I hadn't given him any details about what I had planned.

"Okay," I said to the kids, starting down the Waterfront Trail. "Flashlights on. Let's go."

"A hike?" Kwame said. "We're going on a *hike* in the middle of the night?"

"Not a hike exactly," I said. "You'll see. Just follow me." My kids did follow, walking behind me in perfect single file, and no one pestered me with questions, not even Ian.

We marched onward in the dark for about thirty minutes, with me leading and Otto bringing up the rear. We made it all the way to Kepler's Homestead. But we didn't stop there. And a few minutes later, we came to a giant tree along the left side of the trail.

This was my marker. I'd planned this whole expedition earlier in the day, and I remembered this tree because some of the bark was loose and big strips of it had fallen off. (Only now, in the middle of the night, did I think to wonder *why* the bark was loose: maybe it was because a bear had been sharpening his claws on it!)

I turned away from the tree, toward the undergrowth on the right side of the trail.

"Here," I said, pointing my flashlight into the woods. "In here. But this part gets tricky, so I want you to follow me *very* closely. Walk right in my footsteps. If you don't, I promise that you'll really regret it."

No one said anything, not even Ian. But I could tell that if they didn't find out what was up soon, their curiosity was going to cause them to burst open like seedpods on a Scotch broom plant. Even Otto seemed pretty darn intrigued.

I led everyone twenty or so yards off the trail, into a small clearing. I stopped at last.

"Okay," I said. "Gather in a circle and turn off your flashlights."

Right away, the kids and Otto assembled around me. It took them a little longer to turn off their flashlights, but they did. The stars were blocked by the canopy overhead, so the forest fell into total darkness. (I had planned all this in my mind, but even I hadn't expected it to be so incredibly *black*.)

I didn't say anything for a second, just let everyone absorb the sounds and smells of the night. Finally, I pulled a candle out of my back pocket and lit it with a lighter.

The darkness sprang back from us like vampires from a crucifix. Truthfully, even I was glad to have some light again.

"We're gathered here," I said softly, "for a very important purpose. Now I promise not to hurt you, or make you do anything embarrassing, but before we go any further, I want you all to promise me that you'll never ever tell another person what you're about to hear."

I figured I should go right for the alpha wolf, so I looked at Ian and said, "Well?"

I could tell that he, like everyone else, was dying to know what this was all about. So he nodded yes. A split second later, all the other kids nodded too. Even Otto nodded, which was perfect, because it meant he was taking this just as seriously as the kids.

"Okay," I said into the candle. "Do you all remember the story I told you about Rainbow Crow? And about how the Creator told Rainbow Crow that his new black feathers and his coarse caw were really special gifts?"

Everyone nodded again.

"Well, there's more to the story," I said. "Because those things—black feathers and a ragged voice—didn't always seem like gifts to Rainbow Crow. After a while, the other animals forgot how Rainbow Crow had brought them fire, and they began to laugh and tease the bird. They called him ugly and a freak, and they misjudged him, and sometimes Rainbow Crow felt like he was all alone in the world." The story I was telling now wasn't part of the Native American legend I'd read about. I'd made it up earlier that day. But I figured I was keeping with the spirit of the original story.

"But Rainbow Crow wasn't alone," I continued. "There were other animals who were teased for looking or acting different too. Like the stinky skunk." My kids tittered. "And the ugly turkey. And the blind mole. So Rainbow Crow asked those other animals to join him in a secret meeting in the woods, just like this one. But he wanted it to be a private meeting, so they met in a place where no one would ever go. Does anyone know where that was?"

No one knew.

"Look around you," I said. "What are those plants?"

Everyone squinted into the shadows around us,

but no one said anything for a second. Then Zach said, "Is it poison oak?"

"Yup," I said. "Rainbow Crow and his friends met at night in the middle of a patch of poison oak, because they knew no animal would come upon them there. And they so enjoyed themselves that night that they decided to form a secret society, which they called the Order of the Poison Oak. Then, if anyone ever overheard them talking about it, no one would ever ask to join. Because who would want to be a member of a group called the Order of the Poison Oak? But the name was misleading, because the Order of the Poison Oak was a very special group, and the members all had magic powers. Rainbow Crow had the gift of disguise. Skunk had the gift of his stink-spray. Turkey had the gift of speed. And Mole had the gift of digging."

I paused a moment, then said, as dramatically as I could, "And tonight I brought you here to induct all of you into the Order of the Poison Oak too." Quietly, I added, "'Induct' means to admit someone as a member of a group."

There was another silence. Then Willy piped up, saying, "But how can we be members? We don't have magic powers." (For the record, this was *exactly* the question I'd wanted someone to ask!)

I smiled. "But that's just it. You *do* have magic powers. And it's because of your powers, and the fact that you guys know what it's like to be teased and misjudged, that you're all perfect inductees for the Order of the Poison Oak."

"What powers?" Ian said, but he wasn't being a jerk about it. He just really wanted to know.

"Do you guys know what a scar is?" I asked.

"It's what happens when you get burned," Trevor said.

"Not just burned," I said, thinking of Julian with his acne. "If your skin gets damaged in any way, it grows back thicker and stronger than before, so it can't be hurt again. But when someone has big scars or lots of little scars like you all do, it doesn't just change that part of their skin. It changes all their skin. It makes *magic* skin. It becomes thicker all over. The longer you have scars, the thicker the rest of your skin becomes. It won't be noticeable, and it doesn't protect you from physical stuff, like getting cut with a knife. But it *does* protect you from words. And that means when someone says something nasty about you, calls you a freak, the words can't get through that skin. It can't hurt you underneath."

I looked around in the candlelight; it flickered atmospherically.

"Some of you don't believe me that you have magic skin," I said. "So I'll prove it to you. I want everyone to hold out a hand."

Sure enough, they did. And I pulled some leaves out of my other back pocket.

"I have in my hand some poison oak leaves," I said. "I'm going to give each of you one leaf."

"But I thought you said that our scars won't protect us from stuff like knives!" Kwame said.

"Ordinarily, yes," I said. "Even your thick skin can't protect you from the poison of the poison oak. And you're still not safe from the poison oak all around us. But these poison oak leaves are special. I needed to prove to you that I'm telling the truth about the Order of the Poison Oak. So I had one of Rainbow Crow's descendants make a deal with the plant that these leaves came from. They won't hurt you."

I turned to the kid on my left—Blake. "By accepting this leaf," I said, "you accept membership into the Order of the Poison Oak, and you agree always to be on the lookout for other members of the Order, and to help them whenever possible, but to never reveal to anyone except another member or inductee what you've learned here tonight."

Blake hesitated. Then he reached out and took the

leaf. The other kids all stared at him, at his hand, watching to see if he would break out in a rash.

He didn't. So seven more times, I recited the same words and handed out leaves to the other kids.

Of course, this is where I should confess that I was telling my kids a little fib. We really were in a patch of poison oak, but the leaves I'd been holding weren't really poison oak leaves. No, they were leaves from a plain old oak tree growing back near camp. They were completely harmless. Poison oak looks like oak, and I knew my kids wouldn't be able to tell the difference (they barely even knew what *real* poison oak looked like!).

When I'd passed out leaves to all the kids, Otto said, "Do I get one?"

I smiled. Sure enough, I had one leaf left. I'd brought it for him, even though I hadn't been sure he'd get into the spirit of it all.

Now I inducted Otto into the Order of the Poison Oak too.

When I was finally done passing out the leaves, I went on. "Now, when we get back to our cabins tonight, I want you all to press your leaf between the pages of a book. Then, when it's dry and you get home, I want you to take it and put it somewhere where you'll see it every day, as a reminder of what it means to be a member of the Order of the Poison Oak. Does everyone promise they'll do that?"

The kids and Otto all nodded. I'd never seen a group of ten-year-olds look so serious in my whole life. But that was good. Again, it was just what I'd wanted to happen.

"Okay," I said. "I'm now going to blow out the candle. I want everyone to count to ten before you turn on your flashlights. Then we're going to turn around and walk back to our cabin."

As the kids filed out of that patch of poison oak, Otto walked by me too. I expected him to look at me and wink or smile. And he did look at me, but he wasn't smiling. Even in the feeble light of the flashlights, I could see there were tears in his burgundy eyes.

I'm not much of a baseball player, but earlier that year I had joined the high school baseball team for a few weeks (long story—it had to do with the "bad boy" baseball player I mentioned earlier). Anyway, once I actually hit a home run and won us a game. It had been one of the best, and proudest, moments of my life.

As I led everyone back to camp that night, I listened to the kids buzz with excitement over their induction into the Order of the Poison Oak, and I thought about the tears in Otto's eyes. That's when I realized I had just hit my second home run.

## Chapter Eleven

**The** next morning, I was all smiles. Who wouldn't be? First there was my night with Web two days before. Then there was the thing with the Order of the Poison Oak last night, which would easily win me Counselor of the Decade in any reasonable camp counselor grading system. But when I joined Min for archery, she was all smiles too. In fact, she was so all smiles that she didn't even notice that I was all smiles. Which kind of annoyed me, because it meant that her reasons for being all smiles might be even better than my reasons, and I was still a little sore at Min.

Is all this clear?

Anyway, I said to Min, "You look happy."

"Oh, yeah," she said. There is dreamy-eyed, and there is *dreamy-eyed*. Min was definitely *dreamy-eyed*.

"Why?" I said.

She—of course!—smiled. "Guess."

I didn't want to guess. I wanted her to tell me. And I wasn't all smiles anymore. Because I had this sudden fear that what was making her happy might be the same thing that was making me happy.

"I don't know," I said.

"Web," she breathed.

Bull's-eye! I thought to myself.

"What about him?" I asked awkwardly.

She giggled and leaned closer to me. "We got hot and heavy."

"What?" I said. "When?"

"Last night."

Min was lying—she had to be! Web had said he was gay! Or had he? Maybe he'd just changed the subject. But he *had* said that he and Min were just friends. I was sure of that.

"How hot?" I said. "How heavy?"

"Pretty hot, pretty heavy," Min said. "I mean, we didn't do everything. But we did stuff. Well, mostly *he* did stuff. Which I guess means I'm a slut, but not a whore."

Min and Web *couldn't* have gotten hot and heavy last night, I thought to myself. But the night before, I'd been busy getting things ready for the Order of the Poison Oak, so I had no idea whether Web had been down around the campfire with the other counselors or not.

"So you and Web are still together?" I asked Min.

She looked at me funny. "Of course. Why wouldn't we still be together?"

On the one hand, I wanted to tell her the truth. Something was going on here, and we both needed to figure out what it was. On the other hand, telling her the truth meant telling her something that made me look really, really bad. Web had *told* me that he and Min were just friends! But I was pretty sure that wouldn't make any difference to Min.

Before I told Min the truth, I needed to talk to Web. There were all kinds of possible explanations as to why what happened had happened. Maybe Min and Web broke up three days ago, then he and I got together for a night, then he and Min got back together again. Or maybe Min and Web had been together all along, but they'd also agreed to see other people. But the problem with both these explanations was that Web had told me that he and Min had always only been just friends.

It was Min. I was back to thinking she was lying about Web. But why? That was another thing I needed to talk to Web about.

"Russel?" Min said.

"Huh?" I said.

She repeated her question from a couple of seconds before: "Why wouldn't Web and I be together?"

"Oh," I said. "Nothing. I just hadn't heard you talk about him in a few days. But that's great. I'm happy for you. Really."

The instructor called to us right after that, and I suppose this would be a good place to make some archery reference about how I'd finally felt the pain of Cupid shooting me with his arrow. But that seems stupid. So I'll just end by saying I'd gone from being all smiles to feeling like absolute shit.

Have you ever *really* needed to pee, but you're in some place—an airplane during landing, a freeway with no exit—where going to the bathroom is impossible? That's the way it felt with me wanting to talk to Web. I really, *really* needed to talk to him. But I couldn't leave the archery session, and I knew Web couldn't leave beadworking. So I tried to put the whole me-Web-Min thing completely out of my mind, which was about as easy as ignoring your bladder when you really need to pee.

But lunchtime came eventually, and I hurried back to my cabin to meet my kids, then hustled them all over to the lodge.

Problem was, Web wasn't there. (To continue with the really-having-to-pee analogy, this was like finally finding a bathroom only to see a padlock on the door!)

I got my kids settled at a table, but kept a keen lookout for Web.

Em stepped up beside me. "Did you see we're going out on a pontoon boat for today's all-camp activity?" she asked me.

"Yeah?" I said, trying to pay attention to her but still looking around for Web. "Great."

"But they can only fit two cabins of kids on the boat at a time," Em said. "So we're going in shifts. Meanwhile, the rest of us'll play volleyball."

"I guess that makes sense. Don't want the boat to sink."

"You're up first on the boat. Your kids, and Gunnar's. I saw your names on the list."

"Oh."

"You know," Em said, musing aloud, "I was thinking of taking my kids on a little hike this afternoon. Would you mind if we traded?"

I scanned the cafeteria again, but there was still no Web. "What?" I said to Em.

"Would you care if my cabin went with Gunnar's?

You can go with Otto's cabin, when I was supposed to go. You'd be second."

Suddenly, I spotted Web! He was just entering with his kids.

"I gotta go!" I said.

"Is that okay?" Em asked.

I looked back at her. "Huh?"

"If we trade! My cabin goes first on the pontoon boat, your cabin goes second."

"Sure!" I said. "Whatever."

Out of the corner of my eye, I saw Em smile to herself, but I didn't pay much attention because I was already working my way over to Web.

He was staking out a table with his kids. I pulled him aside. "We need to talk," I whispered.

"About what?" He wasn't whispering at all, which surprised me a little. Maybe it meant he really didn't have anything to hide.

"About Min!" I whispered.

"What about her?" He said this completely casually, like he had no idea what I was talking about. Either that or he was partially autistic.

That's when it occurred to me: we couldn't talk here either. People would overhear. *Min* might see. I glanced around to see if she'd arrived with her kids yet, but she hadn't.

"Never mind," I said to Web. "Let's meet tonight after lights-out. At the cove?"

He grinned at me. "Sure."

In other words, it would be another eight hours before I could finally take a piss!

After lunch, my kids and I headed back to our cabin before volleyball. I brought up the rear, but soon Ian lagged behind with me.

"That was cool," he said quietly, looking over at the lake.

"Huh?" I said.

"Last night in the woods. The Order of the Poison Oak? That was one of the coolest things I've ever done."

"Oh," I said. "Well, thanks." Needing to talk to Web or not, I was all smiles again, at least on the inside.

The kids in front of us had reached our cabin and were going inside, but Ian stopped outside. "I just have one question," he said.

I stopped too and looked at him. "Sure," I said.

"How come you're a member?"

"What?" Suddenly, I wasn't smiling on the inside anymore. Can a person *frown* on the inside?

"You heard me," Ian said. "How come you're a

member of the Order of the Poison Oak? You're not like Otto. You don't have scars."

"Oh," I said. If the qualification for being a member of the Order was that you knew what it was like to be teased and misjudged, well, let's just say my membership papers were in good shape. But I was a member because I was gay, and that was something I couldn't tell Ian.

"Well," I said, stalling for time, "I have psychological scars." *Psychological scars?* Had I really just said something that stupid, especially to a ten-year-old boy? "Let's just say I'm an *honorary* member," I went on quickly. "Okay?"

"Why?" Ian said.

"Why what?"

"Why are you an honorary member? You told us a member can't talk about the Order with anyone except another member. So who talked to you?"

"That's a good question," I said. Problem was, I didn't have a good answer.

"I think I know."

"You do?" I was afraid to ask the rest, but I didn't have much choice. "Why?"

He kicked a pinecone. "You're gay," he said simply.

I had told myself I wasn't going to come out at camp—that the whole point of coming here was to be somewhere where I didn't have to be known as The Gay Kid. But I couldn't lie to Ian. Not after everything I'd said about hidden beauty and not being ashamed of who you are.

The pinecone Ian had kicked skittered to a stop.

"Yeah," I said. "I am."

Ian nodded. "I figured."

I was tempted to ask how he figured, but I didn't.

"You know how I got these scars?" he asked me, tilting his head a little, meaning his melted skin.

"No," I said. "No one ever told me that."

He stared out at the lake. "I was seven years old, at day care after school. My mom hadn't picked me up yet, and I was the only kid left, along with the teacher. All of a sudden, there was this big boom, and the whole building shook, and there were all these weird creaky groans. We knew something really bad had happened, so we ran out into the hallway. I wanted to run out the front doors. But the teacher thought we were in the middle of an earthquake, and the front doors were made of glass and they were by some windows too. So she told me to stop. She was the teacher, so I listened to her. The building kept rumbling, so she told me to get to one side of the hallway. I did everything she said. And that's when steam burst out of the radiator, right into my face." I watched Ian as he told his story. He didn't sound upset. Then again, it wasn't Lake Serenity that I saw reflected in his eyes.

"Wow," I said. "That really sucks."

"I'm not mad it happened," Ian said. He looked at me, and the lake in his eyes had become a raging ocean. "I'm mad I listened to her."

We stared at each other for a second.

"Thanks," I said. "Thanks for telling me."

He nodded once. "Sure. And by the way, it's cool. I won't tell anyone about you."


My kids and I played volleyball until it came our turn to ride the pontoon boat. When we saw the boat returning to the dock, I led them down there.

As the first group of riders was disembarking onto the dock, I noticed something strange. Gunnar looked wet.

Completely wet. Hair and clothes and everything. He was absolutely dripping.

I met him at the end of the dock. "Gunnar? What is it? What happened?"

He didn't look at me. It was almost like he was ignoring me. "Let's go!" he said to his kids, who were snickering amongst themselves. "Everyone to the volley-ball nets! No, leave your life jackets on the boat! I'll join you at the nets in a few minutes!"

"Gunnar?" I said.

"I fell in," he said to me. His kids were on their way to the volleyball nets, and my kids were out on the dock climbing onto the pontoon boat. So we were more or less alone now. But he still wasn't looking at me.

"What?" I said.

"I fell off the pontoon boat!"

I didn't quite know what to say to this. "Well, are you okay?"

He turned on me suddenly. "Maybe you didn't hear me! I fell off the pontoon boat! Right in front of my kids! Right in front of Em. Do you *think* I'm okay?"

"Oh, God, Gunnar. I'm sorry."

"I made a complete fool of myself!"

I glanced out at the boat. It was mostly loaded now. I needed to be out with my kids. "Gunnar, I'm really sorry."

"So?" he said evenly.

"So what?"

"So I thought I was going out on that pontoon boat with your kids and *you*! I saw the list earlier!"

"Oh," I said, remembering. "Yeah. Em wanted to switch. She asked me about it at lunch." And in the back of my mind, I immediately thought, Uh-oh!

"Russ, I thought I asked you not to try to set

me up with Em again!"

"You did. But that's not what this was. Em said she wanted to switch." Of course, now I realized *why* she wanted to switch. She wanted to be able to spend some time with Gunnar, but she hadn't said that outright, because she knew I would have turned her down. I should have turned her down anyway, but when she'd talked to me, I'd been distracted, looking for Web.

"I specifically told you!" Gunnar said. "Twice! And you didn't listen! And I made a complete fool out of myself again!"

"Gunnar, I was distracted, and I—"

He shook his head. "I don't care. I don't want your excuses. Not another word. Because you and I aren't friends anymore."

"What?"

He was already walking away. "You heard me! We're through!"

I'd been at camp less than two weeks, and I'd somehow managed to betray both my best friends. That had to be some kind of record. But I'd waited all day to hear what Web had to say about Min, so that night, after lights-out, I went to meet him at the Cove of the Ever-Changing Rock Formation (tonight the rock looked like Devils Tower, Wyoming—the place in that movie *Close Encounters of the Third Kind*).

I guess he had forgotten that we were there to talk, because the first thing he said was, "Come on! Let's skinny-dip!"

"Wait!" I said. "I wanted to meet here to ask you some questions."

He stopped, his shirt already halfway off. I could see the ridges on his stomach, but not the elastic of his underwear (was he not wearing any again?). Across the lake, forest fires burned, still out of sight, but they must have been brighter now, because tonight they were making the sky throb and ripple like the orange glow of a fake fireplace.

"Shoot," he said.

"Are you with Min or not?"

"What?"

"You heard me."

He dropped his T-shirt back down around his torso. "I told you. No."

"Why does she keep saying you are?"

He arched his back and swung his arms in circles, like he was on a swim team and loosening up for a meet. "Beats me. Maybe she's got a thing for me."

"Were you with her last night?" I asked.

I could see him choosing his words. "For a while,"

he said. "We went for a walk. But it was nothin'."

"Web. I need to know the truth."

"I just told you! She's into me. I tried to tell her I'm not into her, but she doesn't get it."

Something about Web's story didn't seem right. And why did he suddenly sound so impatient with me? On the other hand, it was close to what I wanted to hear. It did kind of make things make sense.

"You need to talk to her again," I said. "Tell her the truth."

He stepped toward me. "I will," he said softly. "Later."

"Wait! This thing with Min!"

"What about it?" He was breathing in my ear.

"It's all a misunderstanding?" I said.

"Oh, yeah. Definitely."

"But—"

"Shhhh." Then he leaned closer to me still and whispered something.

"Web!" I said, even as my pulse quickened.

"What?" He looked absolutely innocent, which was saying something given what he'd just whispered in my ear.

"We can't!" I said.

"Why not?"

"Well, for one thing, we don't have any condoms.

And even if we did, that's just not something I'd do—not for a long, long time."

"What, don't you trust me?"

"No! I barely even *know* you! And you don't know me either. You don't know anything about what I've done and who I've been with."

"Who says I don't know you?" Web said. "I know what kind of person you are. I know all I need to know just by looking in your eyes." And speaking of looking into eyes, that's what he was doing right then.

"Web—"

"I know what a good person you are," he went on. Then he smirked. "And how sexy you are."

I'm embarrassed to say that talk like that from another guy generally works on me. Maybe it *always* works on me, because it was working on me even then.

"Come on." I said this bashfully, like I wanted him to stop, but what I really wanted was for him to go on talking.

Web read me right (not difficult). "You *are*," he said. "The first time I saw you, I thought you were so cute. I knew what I wanted. I wanted . . . *this*."

And he leaned in to kiss me.

The second his lips touched mine, I heard a third

voice, and not in my head.

"Uh-huh!" it said.

Web and I turned to look.

Of course, it was Min.

"Did you *really* think I wouldn't follow you?" she said. I wasn't sure who she was saying this to, Web or me, but I guess it didn't really matter.

"Min," I started to say.

But she, like Gunnar earlier in the day, was already storming away from me.

## Chapter Twelve

**"Min!"** I called after her. "Wait!"

She didn't wait, and I can't say I blamed her. I wanted to follow her, but I wasn't sure what I'd say. Deep down, I guess I'd known that Web was lying about not having been with Min. So what was I doing kissing him? (Though, in my defense, technically *he* was kissing *me*.)

I looked at Web. "Well?"

"Well what?" he said, clueless to the end—or at least pretending to be.

I pushed away, then stood there glaring at him like a disgruntled store detective. "Why is Min so upset?"

"Got me."

"Web!"

"*What?* She's jealous! I told you she's got a thing for me."

"You hooked up with her last night!" I said. "Didn't you?" I sounded accusatory, because I was.

He stared at me for a second. Then he sighed, wilting like a plant. "Okay, I lied. I *was* with Min. I'm sorry, okay? But I had a reason."

"What reason?" There was nothing he could possibly say to excuse what he'd done. Was there?

"I didn't know I was gay," Web said, softly, haltingly. "Not until two nights ago with you. It took me by surprise. I'd never felt that way about a guy before. I *was* with Min then—I lied to you about that. I've been with lots of girls. But it was so different with you. So much better."

"If it was so much better," I said, "what were you doing with Min last night?"

"This is a big deal for me, okay? I'm gay! Like I said, I'd never even thought about that before."

"What does that have to do with—?"

"I needed to know for sure," Web said. "So I hooked up with Min again. I know that's not fair to you, or to Min. But I was confused. I wanted answers. And I found them. By being with Min, I learned once and for all that I didn't want her, or any girl. I want you."

Web sounded absolutely convincing. And even

now, part of me wanted to believe him. Fortunately, I'm not a complete idiot. For one thing, if he didn't know he was gay until that night with me, how did he know he wanted to kiss me the first time he saw me?

"I don't believe you!" I said.

Web looked devastated, like a tree that had been toppled by a windstorm. "I'm telling you the truth! Russel, don't you see? I *love* you."

And that's when I had my answer. He suddenly sounded so unbelievably phony. Up until now, his performance had been pretty damn good. His saying he "loved" me was the first completely false note. But that's how I knew once and for all that this *was* a performance. Web was lying to me, just like he'd been lying all along.

"You're pathetic," I said, turning to go.

"Russel?" Web said. "Please. Don't just walk away. I need you!"

"Would you stop?" I said. "It's not working."

And so Web did stop. He stopped looking like a toppled tree, or even a wilted plant. He stood up taller, but seemed looser, more relaxed. His face lost the hangdog expression too. The change was quick, and so complete that I felt a little like I was watching him transform into a werewolf.

Then he started laughing. Not at me necessarily. Just laughing.

"What?" I said.

"You look so serious!" he said.

Okay, so maybe Web *was* laughing at me. I liked it better before, when he was telling me how sexy I was. I now felt completely self-conscious, but I tried to carry on. "This *is* serious!" I said.

"No, it isn't," Web said. "We were just having fun anyway."

"You just said you loved me!"

"Oh, that."

"Yeah, that!"

"Come on, Russel. That was just stuff."

This guy was incredible! "'Stuff'?" I said. "Did you tell Min that 'stuff' too? That you loved her?"

"Maybe."

"Why?"

"I told you. To have some fun."

"So what are you?" I asked. "Bi?"

"Who cares? I just like sex."

"Why me?"

"Because I could tell you were mooning over me. Dude, you were, like, kinda obvious."

I knew my face was turning red. My only hope was that it wouldn't be visible in the moonlight.

"Then Min told me you were into guys," Web went on. "So I wanted to see just how far I could get. Which was pretty damn far!"

Even as embarrassed as I was, I couldn't help but think: Min had told Web I was gay? How *could* she!

"What kind of person *are* you?" I said. "Lying to people? Taking advantage of them?"

"'Taking advantage'?" Web said. "Are you kidding? It took me all of twenty minutes to get into your pants. Not exactly a challenge. Even Min took longer than that."

By now, Web had to be able to see how red my face was, even in the dark, even in the orange throb of those distant forest fires.

Web laughed again. "Now you don't just look serious—now you look shocked! Hey, it's no big deal. It's the way of the world. Guys need sex. You know I'm right." He held a hand out toward me. "Now come on, let's get each other off!"

I took a step backward, away from him.

"Oh, please!" he said. "It's not like you're Mr. Innocent!"

"What's that supposed to mean?" I asked.

"You knew Min and I were together when you let me put the moves on you."

"I did *not*!"

"Come *on*! You *watched* us."

This was something I hadn't expected him to say. Web knew that I'd watched him and Min skinny-dip?

"What?" I said lamely.

"You know what I'm talkin' about."

"No, I don't! I don't have any idea what you're talking about!"

But Web started laughing again, and that's when I realized that the Order of the Poison Oak was something of a lie. Maybe I did have psychological scars, and maybe they *had* given me thick skin—just like Leo the Lion in that story that Web had told me about Hercules. But it hadn't mattered, because Web, like Hercules, had found a way around my impenetrable skin. He had strangled me with his words and was now slicing me wide open with his laughter.

I had to find Min—to apologize, but also to have it out with her for telling Web about my being gay. Mostly, though, I needed someone to talk to about Web, and she was the closest thing to a friend I had left.

I hurtled down the trail, back toward camp. In the darkness, I kept stumbling on roots and rocks. As much as I wanted to find Min, I wanted even more to get away from Web. I felt like some character in a movie trying to outrun the monster. (The smolder of those distant forest fires made things even creepier, which didn't help.)

Just as I reached the camp area, I ran smack into someone. I hit them so hard that we both fell over, into the bushes.

"Oh, shit!" I said. "Sorry!"

The person next to me on the ground groaned. They'd been carrying a flashlight, which I had somehow not seen, and it was lying near us in the leaves.

"Are you okay?" I said.

"Yeah," said the person. "I think." Otto.

"Oh, man," I said. "I'm sorry. I didn't even see you!"

"It's okay," he said, struggling upright, shaking his head. "Why were you running so fast?"

For one brief second, I had forgotten what had happened back on the beach. Now I remembered.

I started crying, right there in the undergrowth. Right in front of Otto and everything.

"Russel?" he said. "Are you okay? Are you hurt?"

I tried to stop crying, but I couldn't. I just couldn't. It was a cloudburst of the face.

"Here," Otto said, trying to help me upright. "Let's go wake up the nurse."

"No!" I said. I wiped my eyes on my T-shirt, even as they kept leaking tears. "I'm not hurt. It's not the collision. It's something else. Something that happened. The reason why I was running so fast."

"Oh." He hesitated a second. "Well, you wanna tell me about it?"

I did need to tell someone, and I wasn't sure Min would want to see me right then even if I could find her in the dark.

"Yeah," I said to Otto.

It was only then that I realized Web was probably right behind me on the trail. Even now, he was probably listening to me cry, and laughing.

"But not here," I said, wiping my eyes again. This time, they stayed dry. "Let's go somewhere else."

I led Otto to the boathouse. I figured Web would never look for me there, and it was far enough from the fire pit that the other counselors wouldn't overhear us either.

The lake seemed absolutely calm, but somehow I could still hear water lapping quietly against the pilings under the dock. Across the lake, the sky seemed less orange now, and I wondered if it was because the fires were dying down again.

"It's a long story," I said to Otto. He was sitting on the edge of one of the rowboats, and I was pacing back and forth (being careful to avoid sparrow droppings). "Well, it's not really that long. But it's kind of surprising. It's about me and Web. You see, I'm gay."

"I know," he said.

"What?" I said. But my surprise quickly turned to panic. "Wait! Are people talking about me?"

"No," Otto said. "It was last night. Those things you said about the Order of the Poison Oak. They were so beautiful, they made me cry. But afterward, I thought to myself, How could he know those things? You're not a burn survivor."

"So how could I be a member of the Order of the Poison Oak?"

He nodded. "Right. But as soon as I thought about it, I knew the answer."

First Ian, now Otto. I guess I'd been more revealing than I'd thought last night in the woods.

"So you're okay with it?" I asked him.

"That you're gay? Sure. I mean, I have gay friends. Well, one."

So I told him the whole convoluted story of me and Web. I may have left out the part about my spying on him and Min, but only because it slipped my mind at the time.

When I was done, he said, "Wow."

"I know," I said. "I'm such an idiot! How could

anyone be such an idiot to fall for his lies?"

"You're not an idiot. Web's hot."

"Well, so what? Just because someone is good-looking, that doesn't mean everything they say is true!" I was so fired up about everything that had happened that I hadn't quite heard what Otto said. It took me a second to realize that Otto, this presumably straight guy, had just commented on how he thought another guy was hot.

"Wait," I said. "You think Web is hot?" Maybe this wasn't any big deal. But maybe it was.

Otto stood up and walked to the edge of one of the boat slips, then looked out across the lake. "I guess."

"What are you saying?"

"I guess I'm saying what you think I'm saying."

"You're—?"

He nodded. "I mean, I guess."

"But—"

"What?"

I had been going to say, But you're a burn survivor, which would have been remarkably stupid, even for me.

So instead, I said, "Why didn't you tell anyone?"

"*You* didn't tell anyone."

"Good point."

Ironically, talking to Otto really was making me

feel better. Just not for the reasons I thought it would.

"Was Web your first?" Otto asked.

"What? Oh, no. Second." I looked at him. "What about you? Do you have a boyfriend? Is that the one gay person you know?" I wasn't sure if I should have asked this or not, given his scars, which made the question seem weird.

Otto shook his head. "Nah. My gay friend's a girl. I've never been with anyone."

"Oh," I said. "Well, at this point, I'd say you're probably better off."

"Really?"

"I don't know. Maybe I've just had bad luck." I stopped. This felt weird too, complaining about my love life when I'd hooked up with two guys and Otto had never even been with one.

"Well, there is one guy," Otto said.

"Yeah? Here at camp?"

Otto nodded, and that made me curious. There were only so many guys to go around. Five, in fact— at least among the counselors. And if Otto was one and Web and Gunnar and I were out, then who was left? A guy named Bill, who seemed pretty straight. And there was Ryan, one of the camp's two burn survivor advisors. He was in his thirties, but he seemed nice enough.

"Who is it?" I asked Otto.

"Oh, God!" Otto said. "The timing is all wrong! This isn't how I thought it would be. You're all upset about Web and everything."

"Otto. Who is it?"

And with that, he stepped forward and kissed me. It was soft and rough at the same time, and I don't just mean his skin. He was gentle and passionate at the same time too. He smelled like clean pajamas.

Me? Otto liked *me*?

Was this the night for surprises or what?

Finally, he stepped back and watched my face. I felt like a thing of unpopped Jiffy Pop, with him waiting to see if anything would happen.

"Me?" I said at last. "*I'm* the guy you like?"

He turned away again. "I told you the timing was lousy! Oh, hell, it's not about timing, is it? That was so stupid!" He started to leave. "Forget it. Forget I did that, okay? I'm sorry."

"Otto, wait."

He stopped but didn't look at me. Now I could tell that *he* was embarrassed—even in the dark, in the flush of the faraway fires.

"That was nice," I said. "Really nice. It might even be my best kiss ever, because it came when I least expected it, but probably when I needed it most."

He peeked over at me. "Really? You're not grossed out?"

I smiled. That sounded like something I'd say after I kissed some guy. It just made me like Otto more.

"I'm not grossed out," I said.

"So," Otto said. "What do you wanna do now?" Subtle, this guy was not.

"Can we talk for a while?"

"Sure!"

And so we did. But later, we may have kissed some more too.

## Chapter Thirteen

**It** was really windy the next morning—the kind of blustery day when it seems like the whole world is being shaken up like a Boggle tray and it's impossible to predict how everything will end up.

We didn't have an all-camp activity that day. It was already Wednesday, and that first two-week session was ending on Saturday. So each cabin was given the last three afternoons to prepare a skit for the session's wrap-up celebration, to take place that Friday night.

For our skit, I'd decided to have us act out the story of Rainbow Crow (but only the actual Indian legend, not the part I'd made up about the Order of the Poison Oak). I was going to narrate, and the kids were going to dress up like the various animals and the Creator. I knew this was dicey as a camp skit for a couple of reasons. First, there was the whole "fire" issue: did I really want to tell the story of the birth of fire to a group of burn survivors? But the tale had gone over well with my kids, so I figured we should just go for it. I was more worried about the fact that we were doing an actual mini-play, not like the other cabins, which I knew would just be doing silly sketches making fun of Mr. Whittle. The skit I had planned *did* have plenty of humor (for example, when Rainbow Crow tried to get the Creator's attention, he was going to sing the Rolling Stones' "I Can't Get No Satisfaction"). But—and maybe this was the gay boy "artiste" in me—I really wanted our skit to have an actual story, and a point too.

As we worked on the costumes—and our cool fake fire torch!—I remembered something I'd been meaning to tell my kids.

"I'm supposed to pick an Outstanding Camper," I said to them. "Mr. Whittle told us counselors that at the beginning of the year. Each counselor has to pick the Outstanding Camper from his own cabin. I didn't think anything about it at the time. But now that I've gotten to know you guys, I see how stupid it is. I like all you guys—even if your medicines do stink up the cabin at night." At this, I smiled and winked. "Anyway, we're a team, and I don't want to single one of you out." I didn't say the rest of what I was thinking, which was that, in a way, I even loved these guys. It hadn't been two weeks yet, but I felt like I knew everything about them—from Julian's love of trading card games to the fact that Ian was always losing things (not just his flashlight!).

"But I have to pick one of you," I went on. "So I picked the guy who I think everyone will agree had the best attitude all session long, and who was probably the easiest to be around. I picked Trevor."

"Me?" Trevor said.

"Sure," I said. "And I don't mean to act like it's not any big deal. I really appreciate what a good guy you've been, and if anyone deserves this award, it's you. I hope it makes your parents really proud. Anyway, I wanted you guys to know so there wouldn't be any suspense on Friday."

Trevor didn't say anything. But before I could ask how it made him feel, Mr. Whittle appeared from out of the trees. I knew he came around once a day for cabin inspection, but that was always during lunchtime. I'd never known him to come in the afternoon.

"Hey, Mr. Whittle!" I said. "What can we do for you?"

He nodded at my kids but didn't really smile.

"Russel," he said. "I need to see you for a minute, okay?"

"Uh, sure," I said. I looked at my kids. "Just keeping working on the costumes. I'll be right back." Then I let Mr. Whittle lead me away from the others. "What's up?" I said to him.

"We just had a warning from a ranger," he said. "The fires are moving closer, and they're worried about them jumping the lake, what with the wind and all." I glanced over at the water. I didn't see any sign of fire on the opposite shore. And ironically, the smoky haze that had been hanging in the air for days now was gone—but that was probably only because it had been swept away by the wind. "There's no immediate danger," Mr. Whittle went on. "But we don't want to take any chances. So we're going to evacuate the camp, okay?"

I looked back at Mr. Whittle. "Evacuate?"

"It's not as big a deal as it sounds. We're going to move the kids into town, and we can all stay in the high school gymnasium until their parents come pick them up. We're calling the parents now. All this really means is that we have to end the session a couple of days early."

"Oh," I said. It's a little embarrassing that my first thought was, Does this mean we won't be able to do our skit about Rainbow Crow? But I didn't say that to Mr. Whittle. Instead, I asked, "So what do I need to do?"

"Get everyone packed up and ready to go. We want everyone on the buses by three o'clock, okay?"

I nodded. "I can do that."

"But Russel."

I had already started to turn back to my kids, who I just knew were watching Mr. Whittle and me like hawks. "Yeah?"

He lowered his voice. "As I said, there's absolutely no danger. This is all just a precaution. But let's not mention the fire to them, okay? I don't want anyone getting scared. These kids especially. Let's just tell them there's a hurricane coming."

"A hurricane?" I said. "In the mountains?" It made sense to lie, these kids being burn survivors and all. But couldn't we come up with a better lie than *that*?

"Just do it, okay?"

Mr. Whittle left to go tell the other counselors, and I returned to my kids. They were absolutely silent, with all eyes on me, and I knew I'd been right about them watching Mr. Whittle and me.

"It's no big deal," I explained to them. "But the camp session's going to be ending a little earlier than usual. I guess there's been a hurricane warning."

Then, before anyone could question that too closely, I went on to tell them that we had to go stay in the high school gymnasium for a night or two, until their parents came to pick them up. "But it'll be fun at the gymnasium!" I said, trying to keep things light. "It'll be like a big slumber party."

"What about our skit?" Blake asked, and I don't think I'd ever felt so close to a kid in my whole entire life.

"Why don't we bring the props and costumes with us into town?" I said. "I bet we'll still get a chance to do the skit."

"When do we leave?" Zach said.

"In an hour. But you won't be coming back here again, so I need you all to go inside and get everything packed up."

An hour later, my kids and I gathered with all the other cabins out on the marching field. Except I knew at a glance that someone was missing from my group—two kids, in fact.

"Where are Ian and Trevor?" I said to the others.

No one said anything. My kids all stared at the grass at exactly the same time.

I rolled my eyes. "I'm going back to the cabin to get them. No one move until I get back."

"They're not there," Noah said quietly.

"What do you mean?" I said. "Where are they?"

Again, no one spoke.

"Look," I said. "I don't have time for games. Where are they?"

"They went down the trail," Kwame said.

"Trail?" I said. "What trail?"

Zach pointed south. "That way."

The Waterfront Trail? But that led to the narrowest part of the lake. If the fires were going to use the winds to jump the lake anywhere, that's where it would be!

*"What?"* I said, feeling panic grip me like a wrench around a bolt. "Why?"

"They didn't say," Willy said. "But Ian said they'd be back soon."

This was a *disaster*! Camp Serenity was being threatened by forest fires, and now two of my kids—burn survivors, no less!—were heading right into the potential danger zone! Why in the world would they do that?

Suddenly, I knew. Which meant I also knew where Trevor and Ian were going.

As I searched for Mr. Whittle, I forced myself to relax. Ian and Trevor were in *big* trouble, but they weren't in any real danger. They couldn't be. Mr. Whittle had said there wasn't any danger—that the evacuation was just a precaution.

But what if he'd been lying to me? What if the fire had *already* jumped the lake and that was why it was so important to get the kids away quickly? He certainly hadn't hesitated when it came to lying to the kids!

I couldn't find Mr. Whittle or any other adults, but I didn't have time to search the entire camp. I needed to get to Ian and Trevor. I knew where they were going, and they couldn't have gone too far down the trail by now. If I ran, I was pretty sure I could catch up with them.

I found Gunnar and Min, who had gathered their kids out on the marching field too.

"Two of my kids went down the Waterfront Trail!" I said, practically a shout. "I know where they're going, but I can't find Mr. Whittle, so I need your help!"

To their credit, they didn't act all standoffish, despite my having pissed off both of them. I needed them, and they were right there for me.

"The other counselors and I will watch your kids," Min said. "You guys go see if you can catch them."

Gunnar nodded and stepped up next to me.

"Wait," Em said from nearby. "I'm coming too."

"Me too," Otto said, also stepping forward.

I looked back at Min. "When Mr. Whittle gets here, tell him where we went."

And then Gunnar, Em, Otto, and I ran off across the camp grounds for the trail.

"What's going on?" Otto asked me when we reached the trailhead.

As we ran, I explained to the others my theory of what had happened.

It was that damn Outstanding Camper award. My mistake had been telling Trevor I was giving it to him, and how proud it would make his parents.

Trevor didn't *want* to make his parents proud! As Beautiful People, they resented their scarred son for smudging up the perfect Christmas-card photo that was supposed to be their family. For that, Trevor resented them—who wouldn't? As a result, the last thing in the world he wanted was to make them "proud." If they couldn't accept him for who he was, he wanted to *punish* them. And how would he do that? By going to Kepler's Homestead, a place where the kids had been warned never to go! In fact, now that I was reciting my theory out loud, I even remembered Otto saying to the kids how going to Kepler's Homestead without an adult was so serious that any kid who did it would immediately be reported to his parents and expelled from camp!

As for Ian, he'd gone along with Trevor to try to talk him out of it.

I knew my theory made perfect sense. I had *seen* Trevor's parents act uncomfortable around burn survivors, and I'd seen Trevor act resentful in front of them. I also remembered how quiet he had been when I'd told him about the Outstanding Camper award. As for Ian, I knew how seriously he had taken that Order of the Poison Oak thing. And I had specifically said that part of the Order's code was helping out other members—members like Trevor, who was planning to do something as stupid as going to Kepler's Homestead just to embarrass his parents.

Somehow I knew my theory was right. I knew these kids inside and out, body and soul!

Five minutes later, we ran smack into Trevor on the trail. He'd been running back toward us.

"Oh!" I said, surprised. "You're here! You're okay!"

"Huh?" he said.

"You came back from the Homestead!"

He looked at me like I was crazy. "What homestead? I went after Ian. To stop him. But then I saw the fire, so I turned around."

"Fire?" Otto said. So it *had* already jumped the lake!

"Ian!" I said. That's when I realized—duh!—that Trevor was alone. I froze, puzzled. "But why is *Ian* going to Kepler's Homestead?"

"Why do you keep saying Kepler's Homestead?" Trevor said. "Ian wasn't going *there*."

My theory was wrong? I thought, So much for my knowing my kids inside and out, body and soul!

"Then where?" I said. "Where's Ian?"

He hesitated, glancing at Em and Gunnar.

"Trevor!" I said. "This is really, really important! Whatever it is, you've got to tell me!"

Trevor stepped closer to me and lowered his voice. "To the poison oak patch. He lost his leaf."

"What?" I said, still confused.

"His magic poison oak leaf. He lost it, but he didn't want to leave camp without it. So he went back to get another one."

I clued in at last. None of this had anything to do with Kepler's Homestead (now that I thought about it, how would anyone have known that Trevor was there, anyway?). No, it was about Ian having lost his magic leaf. Actually, I thought, this made a lot more sense than my theory about Trevor and his beautiful parents. I had told my kids to keep those leaves forever, to press them between the pages of a book, and Ian *had* said how important the Order of the Poison Oak was to him. And he definitely tended to lose things!

I turned to Otto. "Take Trevor back to camp. Tell Mr. Whittle what's happened."

He nodded, and the two of them ran off down the trail.

Then I looked at Em and Gunnar. "I know where Ian is. This time, I know I'm right. It's not too much farther. But it sounds like there's fire ahead. This could be dangerous. Are you coming?"

Neither one hesitated an instant.

"I'm in," Gunnar said.

"Me too," Em said.

We started down the trail again.

Ten minutes of hard running later, we reached the fire. It wasn't at all how I imagined it would be, or like a forest fire always is in the movies. It was ahead of us on either side of the trail, but it wasn't one big fire burning everything in sight. Instead, it was a bunch of little fires—a stump burning here, a branch burning there. True, sometimes there were bigger patches of fire. But none of them were connected, except by the fact that all the flames were caught in the same breeze, so they would all blow in the same direction with each new gust of wind. Sparks and floating embers whirled around in that wind like a blizzard of burning snow.

The other thing that surprised me was how loud the fire was. It was a cross between a roar and hiss, like the sound of a white noise machine turned way up high.

Up ahead on the trail, maybe twenty yards away, I could see the giant tree that I had used as a marker the night I'd done the ceremony for the Order of the Poison Oak. If Ian had been coming back here to get a poison oak leaf, he had to be around here somewhere.

"This is it," I said to Gunnar and Em. I pointed off to the right, over by where I thought the patch of poison oak would be. "That's where he was going." What with the sound of the fire, I almost had to shout.

We all scanned the undergrowth. But I didn't see anyone.

"Ian!" I shouted. *"Ian!"*

There wasn't any answer, but I doubted he could hear me anyway over the roar of the flames. Should I go farther down the trail? That would mean entering the fire area. And it wasn't like the trail was some protected pathway—there were plenty of fires burning right on the trail itself, on fallen branches or tree roots. If I was going to go in looking for Ian, that meant walking right among those fires, and that seemed really risky.

Maybe Ian was long gone, I thought. Maybe he'd gotten his leaf before the fire had even spread this far. But then I remembered that Trevor had said he'd seen the fire too, which meant that it had to have spread this far by the time he'd arrived here with Ian. And if Ian *had* found a leaf and headed back for camp, why hadn't we met him on the trail? There was only one Waterfront Trail, and the undergrowth along the lake was too thick for him to go bushwhacking.

The lake! If I were Ian and I'd somehow found myself trapped by a forest fire, I would have headed straight for the water. Once in the lake, I could swim to safety.

Was that it? Had Ian swum to safety? At the point where we were, it was about fifty yards from the trail to the water. The fire must have spread up from the shore, I decided, because there were even more of the little blazes down there.

But even as I scanned the area between the trail and lake, Em was pointing. "There!" she said.

And just twenty or so yards beyond and to the left of the big tree trunk, I saw the unmistakable blue of a T-shirt, topped by the face of a bewildered ten-year-old boy.

# Chapter Fourteen

I turned to Em and Gunnar. "You guys should go get help!" I said.

"Otto went to get help," Gunnar said. "I'm staying with you."

"Me too," Em said.

To tell the truth, this was what I'd hoped they would say.

"I'm going in for him," I said. "And this I *am* doing alone." What went unstated was the rest of the thought: that if things went wrong, I would need Gunnar and Em to rescue *me*.

In my mind, I tried to pick out the clearest path through the fires to Ian. It would mean staying on the trail part of the time, but swerving off it at times too.

"Russ?" Gunnar said.

I glanced over at him.

He put one hand on my arm and squeezed. "Good luck, buddy."

So Gunnar and I were friends again. That was good. What was bad was how solemn he sounded. Gunnar was a pretty serious guy, but I'd never heard him sound like that before. He was like a sergeant in some war movie talking to another soldier right before he leaves on some suicide mission. And the thing was, this was almost that serious. I was trying to save someone from dying. And if something went wrong, I could die too. I'd sure never done anything anywhere near this serious before.

But I wasn't scared. I knew what I had to do. Now it was just a question of doing it, and seeing how things turned out. In fact, in spite of the high stakes—or maybe *because* of them!—I couldn't remember ever being quite so calm. This was worth remembering the next time I got all bent out of shape because I found myself wearing the "wrong" pair of underwear in the locker room after P.E. class.

I nodded to Gunnar, then turned and started running toward Ian. I was immediately reminded of Rainbow Crow and his three-day journey back from the land of the Creator with a burning branch in his beak.

Like Rainbow Crow, I had smoke in my face. It was thick and dirty, and I felt like a vacuum cleaner, sucking in particles of grit and ash. But I was a living vacuum cleaner, so I could also feel and taste the stuff. It scraped the tender linings in my nose and throat, and also stung my eyes.

And like Rainbow Crow, I felt heat. It came at me in waves, these intense blasts unlike anything I had ever experienced before. It was the heat that explained why a green forest was even burning in the first place. After a while, *anything* would catch on fire in heat this strong—not just deadwood and pine pitch, but living wood, ferns, and bushes. Sure enough, little fires were exploding into being all around me (like I really was a soldier on a suicide mission, and was now on the receiving end of enemy artillery).

Eventually, I would burst into flames too. That's what it felt like, anyway. Already I knew I was going to have one hell of a "sunburn." Even the rubber in my tennis shoes was melting, making it feel like I was walking on sticky gum.

The heat was *too* strong—and it looked like the worst of the fire was still ahead. Unlike what the burning torch had done to Rainbow Crow, this fire wouldn't just turn my feathers black. It felt like if I didn't stop, my skin would burst into flames. I thought that would be ironic—that then maybe Otto and I really would end up being the perfect couple.

I couldn't go on. I had to stop. But I'd only just made it to the giant tree trunk—not even halfway to Ian.

I thought about returning to Em and Gunnar and waiting for the firefighters who were sure to come. But they might not be there for an hour or more—not until Otto got someone to call the firefighters and they somehow managed to make it to Camp Serenity, then all the way down the trail. Even the helicopters couldn't save us, because they wouldn't be able to see where we were. But if we had to wait an hour or more for help, Ian would die.

The problem was, if I kept going forward, I would die too. I might have kept going anyway if my dying would save Ian. But it wouldn't. If I went down, he would too, for sure.

I didn't know what to do. Helplessly, I searched the area, as if for an answer. Incredibly, I immediately found the answer I was looking for.

The tree bark! The giant tree that I had used as a marker on the trail a few days before? The bark was loose. Big hunks of it littered the floor of the forest around the base of the trunk. What had Otto said that time about the bark of old-growth trees? That they had fire-retardant properties! Sure enough, none of the pieces of bark were burning.

I picked up the largest scrap of bark I could find and held it up like a shield. It was no help against the smoke, but it did seem to deflect some of the heat.

I started forward again. I found that if I crouched down low while I ran, the heat was less intense, and the smoke wasn't as thick either. My tennis shoes were still melting, but hey, I couldn't have everything.

I reached Ian at last. He wasn't crying, which meant he was more butch than I would have been in his place, especially at age ten. Of course, the heat was so strong that maybe his tears were drying before they even had a chance to fall.

"Are you okay?" I said to him. It was even louder inside the fires than it was at the edge, so this time I really did have to shout.

Ian didn't answer me or even look at me. That's when I wondered if maybe it wasn't that he was so butch. Maybe he was in shock—in some place beyond tears.

"You're going to be okay!" I said to him. "I'm going to carry you out of here!"

He still didn't move, or even react. He looked sad but helpless, like one of those starving children on the commercials for sponsor-a-kid charities.

I squatted down in front of him and threw his limp arms around my neck.

"Hold on to me!" I said, and fortunately he did. Then I reached for my shield of tree bark, which I used to cover us both. With that, I stood up a little—enough to be able to walk, but not so much that I'd have to face the full brunt of the smoke and heat again.

I turned back the way I had come.

A bush exploded into flames in front of me. A fern went up next to it. Then, right in a row, a tree branch flared up like a torch. The fire was spreading, being driven by the wind. But that meant it wasn't just like being on the receiving end of enemy artillery. It was more like being attacked by an evil wizard—like some fire-wielding spell-caster was using magic to cut off my escape. If I tried to walk through these new blazes, I'd be burned for sure.

The fires were blocking me. I couldn't go back the way I'd come.

I turned to the left, in the direction of the poison oak patch, but other fires raged there. It was impassable too.

The lake! I needed to do what Ian had been trying to do and get to the water.

But when I turned in that direction, I saw that the

fires were still thickest there. There was absolutely no way I'd make it the forty yards to the lake.

The whole area was going up in flames, like the forest was a grid and each square was slowly being filled in with fire.

There were blazes all around us now. That meant there was no way out. That meant Ian and I were trapped.

## Chapter Fifteen

**Suddenly**, a great wave of water rolled over the fires in front of me. It splashed everywhere, dousing the nearby flames and even spattering up onto me, cooling the blistering skin on my bare calves and thighs. As water met fire, it created one of the most satisfying noises I'd ever heard—a loud, angry, but quickly fading hiss.

*What in the world*—? I had absolutely no idea what was going on!

But as the steam and smoke cleared, I saw the source of that mysterious and wonderful wave of water. Em and Gunnar were just beyond, standing behind a rusted metal trough, which was now on its side on the ground. They must have run back and grabbed that old trough from Kepler's Homestead, filled it with as much water from the lake as they could carry, and brought it right into the fire. Then they'd poured the contents onto the flames.

Unfortunately, they hadn't put out *all* the fires—just the ones right in front of Ian and me.

"Come on!" Gunnar shouted. "Let's get out of here!"

I didn't need to be told twice.

But as I tractored Ian forward, Gunnar shouted, *"Em!"*

I looked over at where she was standing, several yards to one side of the upturned trough. But the evil fire-wielding wizard was back at work again; little fires leaped up right in front of her.

Now Em was the one who was trapped. But the trough was empty—they'd used all the water to save Ian and me!

Without thinking, Gunnar reached down and lifted the trough up again. Then he turned and slammed it down on top of the fires. Once it was in place, he clambered into it, using it like a bridge across the flames.

When he reached Em, he said, "Are you all right?"

"Huh?" she said. She'd been so surprised by the fires that she was in something of a state of shock now too. So Gunnar didn't say another word. He just grabbed her around the waist and lifted her onto his shoulder—which is saying something, since he isn't known for his upper-body strength. Then he carried her back over the trough-bridge.

"Come on!" he said to me. "We need to get out of here!"

And that's exactly what we did.

Safely away from the fires, Gunnar and I put Em and Ian down in the middle of some bushes.

"Are you okay?" Gunnar asked Em.

"You saved my life," she said. She still looked stunned, but in a good way now.

"Huh?" Gunnar said.

"You saved my life! If not for you, I would have died back there!"

"What? No." We were all red-faced from the heat, but suddenly I think Gunnar's face was a little redder than ours.

"You *did*!" Em said, and the only word I can use to describe her expression is to say she was beaming.

Meanwhile, I turned to Ian. There were signs of life in his eyes now too, but he still wasn't crying, which told me that maybe he was just as butch as I'd thought at first.

"Are *you* okay?" I asked him.

"Yeah," he said. "I'm sorry. That was so stupid!"

"It's okay. It doesn't matter. All that matters is that you're okay."

"I just wanted a leaf," he said. "But I didn't know there was a fire."

"I know. That was my fault. I should've told you."

"I shouldn't have gone in. Trevor told me not to. But when I got there, the fire hadn't spread yet. It was the wind! It was like the fire just surrounded me. It's funny. The last time I listened to someone, my teacher, I got burned by the steam. This time, I didn't listen, and I almost died."

I wasn't about to hug Ian, because I knew that was the last thing he wanted, even now. But I figured I should do or say something that showed him everything was all right. "I'll get you another leaf," I said. "I promise."

"Leaf?" Em said.

"Poison oak," I said. "It's a long story." I looked at Ian and winked. "It's kind of private, anyway."

Em glanced around. "Well, if you're looking for a leaf from a poison oak plant, you won't have to go far."

"What do you mean?" Gunnar said.

"We're sitting in it."

"In what?"

"Um, poison oak."

Em was right. Gunnar and I had escaped the fire, carried Em and Ian out into the woods, and dropped them right into a patch of poisonous plants.

"Oh, God!" Gunnar moaned. "I can't believe it! I actually save someone's life, and what do I do? I carry them into a patch of poison oak. That *so* figures!" I thought this was ironic. Gunnar had just saved all our lives, and now he was embarrassed that he'd led us into some mildly poisonous plants. I guess this was like my not being scared of running into a forest fire to rescue someone, but being terrified of wearing the wrong brand of underwear in P.E. class.

But Em wasn't having any of it. "No!" she said to Gunnar, sharply. "Don't do that! What you did today was brave and great. Don't ruin it by talking like you did something dumb. The poison oak isn't important. It doesn't matter at all."

It did matter a little, of course. When we finally got to the high school gymnasium later that night, the four of us all took long soapy showers, trying to wash off the poison oak resin. But it was too late for Em and Gunnar. By the next morning, their skin had already begun to blister. According to Gunnar, the itching was incredible, and it was weeks before they were finally fully healed.

Interestingly, both Ian and I were completely unaffected by the poison of the plant.

# Epilogue

**For** me, this was the point when the summer finally started to get good. But while everything that happened after that was very exciting for me, it probably wouldn't be all that exciting to read about, because it was mostly happy stuff. And no matter what anyone says, happy stuff is really pretty boring for everyone except the people involved (this is the reason why graduation ceremonies are boring but car crashes aren't, and why newspapers write about floods and robberies, but not sunsets and birthday parties).

Still, there are a few things that happened over the rest of the summer that *aren't* boring, and I figure I should mention them here.

First of all, it finally rained a couple of days after Gunnar, Em, Otto, and I rescued Ian. That put out all the nearby fires, so Camp Serenity was able to go on as if nothing had happened. The four of us were heroes for saving Ian's life, but only for about two days. Then the kids from session one went home (tearful good-byes, etc.) and the next session of kids arrived, and they couldn't have cared less about something that had happened two days before they got there. Mr. Whittle and the other adults and counselors remembered, of course, but they were so busy with the next session of kids that no one ever really mentioned it.

Speaking of the next session of kids, I got a cabin full of little monsters again (and they weren't burn survivors, so they had no excuse). The kids from session three were even worse. My fourth-session kids were fantastic, but the fifth-session ones were little monsters again. In every case (except with my fantastic fourth-session kids), I had to somehow (a) establish myself as an authority figure, and (b) quickly earn their respect. Sometimes I was more successful than other times, and sometimes I'd pull it off only to screw it up a few days later, just like during the first session with Ian, Trevor, and the others. But except for the third session (which was apparently reserved for Rosemary's Baby, Damien, and other spawn of Satan), I always ended up bonding with my kids. In other words, I think I did a pretty damn good job as a summer-camp counselor.

Incidentally, my experience over the rest of the summer made me rethink my opinion of teachers yet again: I was back to thinking that teachers whose classrooms are out of control really are, for the most part, crappy teachers.

As for Gunnar and Em, they finally got together. It helped that they were both in misery from the poison oak, because that meant they spent a lot of time together commiserating, and they ended up bonding over that. Gunnar's rescue of Em helped too. She kept jokingly referring to him as "my hero" for saving her from the flames. At first, this embarrassed Gunnar. But then he started going with the flow, calling her "milady" and "my fair maiden." She responded in kind, calling him "my noble rescuer" and "my fair knight." Before long, they were bowing and curtseying, and tossing flowers and making garlands for each other, and just generally laying it on pretty thick. This went on all summer, and I found it either kind of cute or really sickening, depending on my mood.

Mostly, of course, I was just thrilled that good ol' Gunnar had finally found himself a girlfriend, and a really cool one at that.

* * *

It took a while for Min and me to completely make up. Part of the problem was that neither of us really felt like we'd done anything all that wrong, so neither of us wanted to be the one to come out and apologize. All Min had done was go after a guy she was hot for, even though she had known I was hot for him too. And while I'd let myself be seduced by Web, he'd come after me, not the other way around. And he *had* said at the time that he and Min were just friends. True, I had spied on Min and Web that one night in the Cove of the Ever-Changing Rock Formation, and that was outright, no-excuses wrong on my part, but Min didn't know about that. Besides, Min had also told Web I was gay, and that was wrong too.

One afternoon during the second session, we finally had it out. Ironically enough, we were playing tug-of-war: my cabin against hers. She was the anchor for her kids on one end of the rope, and I was the anchor for my kids on the other end.

We were out on the marching field, tugging each other back and forth, but neither side was managing to pull the other across either of the two chalk lines that marked defeat.

Then, suddenly, Min started shouting out commands, and like little soldiers in pink friendship bracelets, her campers started a steady march backward. Slowly but surely, my side slipped forward toward the dreaded chalk line.

A second later, my side completely crumpled (my second-session kids always were a bunch of pansies). Min's kids fell backward onto the grass, and my kids and I went thundering forward across both chalk lines, falling onto Min's kids, creating one big pile of flailing campers. Somehow, I managed to land right on top of Min.

A few days earlier, I would have immediately rolled away from her, and she would have pulled away from me.

But not then. For some reason, we just lay there laughing. I looked down at her, and she looked up at me, and we smiled. It felt so good to be touching each other that we stayed like that until long after our kids were up on their feet again and moaning at us to get moving.

It may not sound like much, but I knew right then that Min and I were back to being best friends. And sure enough, I was right.

What about Web? Min and I both avoided him like the plague (which, for all we knew, he actually had, the disgusting sleazebag). By the last session, he'd worked his way through most of the counselors (including straight-guy Bill, or so the rumor went). Incredibly, it wasn't until the start of that last session that someone—Lorna, one of his earlier conquests—accused him of sexual harassment. He didn't get sent home or anything, but he did get reprimanded and everyone started avoiding him, and it was all very embarrassing for him and wonderfully gratifying to Min and me. In fact, when the shit started hitting the fan for Web, I don't think Min and I had ever been so close.

Finally, there was Otto and me. That was the best thing about the rest of the summer, because we got together too. (See? I didn't just like "bad boys"!)

What surprised me the most about him was how much we had in common. We liked all the same books and movies and music. More than anything, we thought about things the same way, and we spent hours walking along the beach, talking about everything under the moon. I know that opposites attract, but who the hell wants to spend time with an opposite? What in the world would you talk about?

Some of my best moments from that summer were sitting around the campfire listening to Otto sing. Once he even wrote a song called "Russel's Song," especially about me (this is just about the most flattering thing imaginable). And yes, once or twice we may have gone skinny-dipping ourselves in the Cove of the Ever-Changing Rock Formation.

Eventually, of course, summer came to an end. All that last week, I felt absolutely shitty.

The Friday night before the Saturday we were supposed to leave, Otto and I went for a midnight row out on the lake. He rowed, and I sat in the back, facing him. But tonight, unlike most of our nights together, we barely spoke at all. Now I know what they mean when people talk about unsaid words hanging in the air. It was almost like you could hear the word "good-bye" in the splash of his oars, and echoing off the lake around us. But neither one of us wanted to be the one to say it out loud.

Finally, Otto stopped rowing, and we drifted on the silent water.

"I'll understand if you don't want to see me," he said at last.

"What?" I said.

"Well, camp is ending, and we'll be going home." Otto had come a long way to be a camp counselor for burn survivors. He lived something like eight hundred miles away.

"I know we live far apart," I said. "But we can make it work."

Otto looked out over the water. "Well, yeah, there's that. But the other thing too."

"What other thing?"

"Come on, Russel," he said. "You know."

"No, I don't." For the first time in weeks, I had no idea what he was talking about.

"My scar."

"What scar?"

"Russel."

"You mean the burn scar?"

He nodded in the moonlight.

"What about it?"

"It's just that I know things are different out in the real world."

Even now, it took me a second to understand what he was saying. Remember that first time I listened to Otto play that song around the campfire and suddenly his whole face seemed to change? Well, that's the way he now looked to me all the time. It wasn't that I didn't see the scar. It's just that I thought of it as part of him, as something beautiful. (I'm not mentioning this to make myself seem noble or compassionate. It's just the way it was.)

"You think I won't want to be seen with you in

public because you have a scar?" I said.

"It's not like that," Otto said. "I know you wouldn't act embarrassed or anything. But camp is different. Everyone knows everyone here. It's not like that in the real world. When it comes to boyfriends, I'd understand if you'd rather be with your own kind."

Was he kidding? But even in the dark, I saw on his face that he wasn't. "Otto," I said, "you *are* my own kind! Remember? Order of the Poison Oak?" It made me sad to think that even now, he wasn't sure where I was coming from. But I'd talked with him enough to know that he knew for a fact that pity can make people do amazing things—maybe even spend time with someone for two months when they're not really in love.

For a second, I wasn't sure what else to say. I wanted to stand up in that rowboat and shout that we'd be together forever, because I thought it might make him feel better, and also because that's the way I felt. But that seemed wrong somehow. Promising him my undying love because I thought it would make him feel better was just a variation on the whole dating-him-out-of-pity thing. It was the exact opposite of what he was asking me for. Plus you're never supposed to stand up in a rowboat.

"Otto," I said at last. "I don't know what's going to happen to us as a couple, but I know what I *hope* will happen. I hope we keep seeing each other, maybe even forever. But no matter what does happen, I know I will always be your friend. And that I will always love you."

There, I thought. That was what I wanted to say to him. It wasn't completely pretty, but it was the absolute truth. That was what Otto needed—for me to treat him like anyone else I would love. It had taken me a long time to learn that lesson, but eventually I had gotten it through my thick skull.

Otto stared at me with tears streaking his face. At some point during my little speech, he had started to cry. If the scars on his face made his skin extra thick, it didn't seem that way now. Now it was like there was no skin at all, like I could see right into his very soul. I saw that he was looking at me the way Peppermint Patty had looked at the Little Red-Haired Girl—and the way I had looked at Web that night in the cove. In his eyes, I was perfect.

Sure enough, he said, "Russel! I love you so much!"

Now *I* was crying, because Otto looked perfect to me too. There are tears of sorrow and tears of joy, but these were some weird new kind of tear—tears of sorrow *and* joy. I felt like I was feeling every emotion I'd ever experienced, all at once. If I had been a fuse box, I so would have blown myself out.

Then I was on the seat next to him, holding him and kissing him.

"I'm so glad I met you, Russel Middlebrook," Otto said. "I think I must be the luckiest guy in the world."

"Second luckiest," I said, kissing him again.

You're not supposed to stand in a rowboat, and we didn't. But there are other things you can do, and Otto and I definitely did plenty of those.

The next day, Gunnar, Min, and I drove home. I felt sad and tired, but also oddly relaxed.

"So!" Min said to Gunnar and me. "What was the best part of the summer? And don't say Em or Otto, because my love life sucked this summer, so that would just be mean."

"The chocolate chip pancakes," Gunnar said. "Em was right. They're great."

I thought about what I was going to say. I knew the real answer. It was that night with my kids and Otto when we'd created the Order of the Poison Oak. I never had told Gunnar and Min about that.

And I'd never repeated the induction ceremony with kids from later sessions, no matter how out of control my cabin got. It just didn't seem right.

"Russel?" Min said. "What'd you like best?"

"I don't know," I said. "I guess it's a feeling."

"Oh, God," Gunnar said. "Not a *feeling*."

"Here we go," Min said, rolling her eyes. "Russel's going to get all philosophical on us."

I ignored the fact that I was pouring my heart out and my two best friends were mocking me mercilessly. "It's something I've never felt before," I said. "It started with my kids from that first session—how I kind of won them over. Then there was when we rescued Ian from the fire. And there were my other kids—well, except for the third session. And, well, my whole relationship with Otto—sorry, Min."

" 'Sokay," she said.

"What feeling?" Gunnar asked.

I thought for a second, then said, "Invulnerability. Like I'm Superman. Like there's absolutely nothing that can affect me. Not knives, not bullets, maybe not even Kryptonite."

"I think that's true," Gunnar said. "If that camp food didn't kill you, nothing will."

"Think the feeling'll last?" Min asked me. "I mean,

do you think you'll still feel that way this fall at school?"

I shrugged. "Oh, I don't know. Probably not." But that's just what I said out loud. To myself, I was thinking, Well, maybe a little.

## Acknowledgments

If I could spend a summer in the mountains with my friends, here are some of the people I'd invite: my partner, Michael Jensen; my agent, Jennifer DeChiara; my editor, Steve Fraser; my publicist, Brooke Ford; and my longtime buddies Tom Baer, Tim Cathersal, Danny Oryshchyn, Lynn Sauriol, and Laura South-Oryshchyn. And I'd hope the following folks would at least be able to stop by: Susan Schulman, Victoria Ingham, Margaret Miller, Tui Sutherland, Alison Donalty, Rob Holt, Ali Smith, Janet Frick, Suzanne Daghlian, and Christina Gilbert.

Thanks must go to those who were especially helpful on this particular book: Marcy Rodenborn, who is quickly becoming my go-to gal on all manner of plot questions, and Bret Tiderman, whose memories of his own experiences as a summer-camp counselor were so detailed that it almost felt as if I had been a counselor too.

# THE ORDER OF THE POISON OAK

## From the Desk of Brent Hartinger
### www.brenthartinger.com

Dear Reader:

I hope you enjoyed reading the latest adventures of Russel and his friends Min, Gunnar, Em, and Otto as much as I enjoyed writing them. And now that you *have* read the book, I thought you might be interested in joining the Order of the Poison Oak yourself.

By now, you already know all about the club. What you may not know is that anyone can join. The only qualification? You have to know what it's like to be teased or judged for looking or acting different from other people. The only requirement? You have to keep your eyes open for other people who are being teased or judged for looking or acting different, and you have to try to help them whenever possible.

For the paperback edition of this book, I'm including an official Order of the Poison Oak membership certificate, located at the very end of this "Extras" section. I also recommend finding yourself a real oak leaf (preferably plain old oak, like in the book, not actual poison oak!). Then press that leaf between the pages of a book to dry it, and put it somewhere where you'll see it every day, to remind yourself what it means to be a member of the Order.

There are many ways to judge the value of a human life. But I believe to the core of my being that the very *worst* way to judge another—and the most *inaccurate* way!—is to do it based on something as superficial as the way that person looks, his or her race, religion, or gender, how much that person weighs, or, yes, his or her sexual orientation.

If you took the time to read my book, I suspect you believe that too.

Anyway, welcome to the Order of the Poison Oak! Whoever you are, whatever your difference, be like Rainbow Crow and always fly way up high and very, very proud, okay?

Peace!

Brent Hartinger

P.S. E-mail me at brentsbrain@harbornet.com and tell me why you qualify to be a member of the Order!

Age at which decided to become a novelist: 21

Age at which first published a novel: 37

Weeks it took to write the first draft of *Geography Club*: 3

Weeks it took to write the first draft of *The Order of the Poison Oak*: 12

Largest number of books signed in one sitting: 350

Number of plays written: 12

Number of plays produced: 11

Reason why that one play was never produced: It stunk.

Favorite food: Vietnamese spring rolls with peanut sauce

Least favorite food: squash

Favorite cuisines, in order of preference: Vietnamese, Chinese, Indian, Thai, Mexican, Italian, American

Favorite sound: a purring cat

Least favorite sound: a bratty kid

Guilty pleasure: *Xena: Warrior Princess*

Most desired time-travel destination: Egypt, 2000 B.C.

Second most desired time-travel destination: North America, 75 million years B.C.

Most desired interplanetary travel destination: Europa, the moon of Jupiter

Number of really, really close calls to dying, to
   date: 2
Number of out-of-body experiences, to date: 1
Nightly flosser: yes
Telling the truth about being a nightly flosser: yes
Favorite dessert: fresh fruit
Telling the truth about favorite dessert: no
Real favorite dessert: chocolate fondue

## Brent Hartinger Talks About
### *The Order of the Poison Oak*

**Is Russel Middlebrook you?**
Fiction writers are never supposed to admit that their characters are autobiographical, and it's true that Russel isn't me, exactly. But he thinks like me, acts like me, and looks like me (or at least he looks like I looked in high school). I tried hard to make Russel likeable, which basically means he has all of my good qualities and none of my bad ones.

I'd like to think if you like Russel, you'd probably like me. But if you don't like Russel, I'm positive you wouldn't like me (and I probably wouldn't like you!).

**Why did you write a sequel to Geography Club?**
To tell the truth, I just always assumed I would. Right before *Geography Club* came out in 2003, I mentioned this to my editor. He sort of smiled and said, "Well, let's wait and see how *Geography Club* does, okay?" I guess I didn't know that publishers only publish sequels to *successful* books!

In any event, *Geography Club* did very well, and HarperCollins ended up being very eager for a sequel. I was *happy* to oblige.

**Why isn't the story a continuation of the events in Geography Club?**

Because that story has already been told (and finished!). If it wasn't already in that book, it didn't need to be said.

Here's my take on writing sequels: Everyone thinks they want to read more of the first book's story, but when most people *do* read a sequel that's just more of the same, they usually end up feeling disappointed. I think what people really want from sequels is to once again feel the way the first book made them *feel*. But to keep the new book from seeming repetitive or redundant, I felt I needed a new setting, new secondary characters, new themes, new challenges for Russel and his friends, and unexpected new twists.

Interestingly, once I had finished the first draft and was revising it, I happened to notice that the emotional "beats" of the book were almost exactly the same as *Geography Club*; in other words, even though the story is completely different, the underlying structure is very similar (if you don't believe me, map it out for yourself!). This wasn't a conscious design on my part, so it was kind of eerie to see all the parallels. But I guess subconsciously, this is how I tried to make the book feel comfortable and familiar, despite having a whole new story.

EXTRAS

Did I succeed in writing an effective sequel? That's for the reader to decide.

**Why this particular story?**
I have to admit, part of the reason why I wanted to write a sequel was because I wanted to write a gay teen book that was about something other than how hard it is to be a gay teen. That's kind of been done to death lately. So while the story has a same-sex romance, and Russel's being gay certainly reinforces the theme, the focus is about much more than just his being gay.

Frankly, I think that's the next wave of gay teen lit anyway: the incidentally gay teen. You read it here first!

**Why isn't Kevin from Geography Club in the book?**
That was a tough one. For a long time, he was going to be, but somehow it always felt wrong. I guess, ultimately, I think that his story line was pretty well wrapped up at the end of *Geography Club* (mostly because he is the one character who doesn't really change). Plus, I think he and Russel needed some time apart. I know this disappoints a lot of people, but Kevin will definitely appear in the next book in the series.

**The book shows a new side to Min. What's that about?**
While I adore Min, I wanted people to understand that she isn't Ms. Perfect—that she sometimes makes mistakes too, just like Russel and Gunnar. Meanwhile, I've always felt bad that Gunnar came off so poorly in *Geography Club*, because I believe he is ultimately a decent guy. So I thought it would be interesting if, in the new book, Gunnar got to be the good guy for a change, and Min showed a bit of her darker side. Mix things up a bit.

**The Order of the Poison Oak *is a little steamier than* Geography Club. Why?**
Well, it *is* summer camp, so some skinny-dipping seemed required! As for the rest of it, Russel is getting a little older, a little more sophisticated, and I wanted to explore his maturation a little bit. Plus, I wanted to touch briefly upon the notion of safer sex. It all seemed very appropriate to the story.

**Why are there almost no adults in *Geography Club *and* The Order of the Poison Oak?***
I deliberately chose to remove almost all adults from the books, because I always saw these books as being about the moral choices of teenagers, and I frankly think most of those choices are made

9

outside the presence of adults. But I was also trying to recreate the experience of being a teenager, where it often seemed to me that the only thing that mattered was the opinion of my peers. This is also the reason why I never specify a town or state: The stories exist out of time and out of place, in the isolated bubble that is the teenage years.

I've been criticized by some for taking the adults out of the books, but I have no regrets. The way I see it, a lot of adults are threatened by the fact that they don't appear in my book, but no one ever gets upset by the fact that there are plenty of books about adults that include no teenagers whatsoever.

And a lot of adults must agree with my take on things. I have many adult crossover readers.

**Have your books ever been challenged?**
Repeatedly. Apparently, there is a group of people that not only wants to decide what they and their kids are reading, they also want to decide what *everyone else* reads too. In all the challenges that I know of, these people have not been successful in getting my book removed from school or public libraries, mostly because courageous librarians took a stand. But I'm sure there are lots of cases that I never hear about where the self-appointed censors won, and the book was removed (and

burned?), and I know there are many other cases in which the librarian was too afraid to buy my books in the first place.

You know, you really have to hate or fear a book to want it removed from a library, and it feels horrible to be the object of that hate. Intellectually, you know it's not about your book at all, it's about *their* political agenda. But there is a frustration on the part of all the writers I know who have been challenged, an eagerness to engage in some kind of "good faith" dialogue that is simply not possible with a lot of the folks on the other side.

I believe books like mine have a place in the world. In the past two years, I've received thousands of e-mails and letters from teenagers and adults thrilled that my books exist. In some cases— and I'm so not trying to brag, because it's really not about my book at all—it seems to have even kept kids from killing themselves.

**Did you ever go to summer camp?**
Like Russel, I only went to day camp. I was never a camp counselor either. Fortunately, my friend Bret Tiderman (who I met while on tour for *Geography Club*) was a camp counselor for many years, and he was able to provide me with all the necessary details.

### Is the Rainbow Crow story a real legend?

Definitely! Again, being summer camp, an Indian legend seemed required. I found this one in a book called *The Grandfathers Speak: Native American Folk Tales of the Lenape People* by Hitakonanu'laxk. I thought it was an extremely moving story, and there was literally a spot in my manuscript outline that said, "To distract them from the forest fires, Russel tells the kids an Indian legend." I was shocked by how perfectly this particular legend fit into my existing story line (which already involved burn survivors), and my theme (which was already about how true beauty lies within).

I only added the part that Russel himself adds, about the Order of the Poison Oak.

### What's the song that Otto sings around the campfire?

Well, it was going to be "Landslide" by Stevie Nicks, but she wouldn't give us the rights to reprint the lyrics. So then it was going to be "I Believe in Love" by the Dixie Chicks. Things were all set to go, but at the last minute, there was a legal problem, and it turned out we couldn't use those lyrics either. So I sat down and wrote a song myself, called "Is It Okay if I Need You Tonight?" While I was at it, I wrote music too!

Frankly, I'm really glad the book ended up with

this song. I think the new song (which, in the book, Otto wrote) tells us a lot more about Otto than either of those other two songs did.

### How can I hear the complete song?
Well, if I ever get the nerve, I'll upload a sound file on my website (www.brenthartinger.com). In the meantime, I've included the sheet music as part of this "Extras" section.

### There will be more books in the Russel Middlebrook series, right?
Definitely! Are you kidding? I love writing these stories, and people seem to enjoy reading them. As long as those two things are true, I'll keep going forever. In short, I'm milking this cash cow till she dies of dehydration!

# Is It Okay if I Need You Tonight?

*words & music*
Brent C. Hartinger

yard and for to-night being a-lone is just too hard.

2. Is it o-kay if
3. Is it o-kay if

I want you to-night? It's a
I love you to-night? I know

ve-ry long time un-til the mor-ning light.
it's way too soon I have no right.

and since we're both here in the dark, can I
The fire is fa-ding in the pit, but the

ask one thing of you? Is there a chance that
spark is in your eyes. Is it o-kay if

(after vs. 3 To Coda)

you might want me too?
I love you to-night?

and it's o-kay if you need me to-

night.

*This certifies that the bearer of this certificate is a member in good standing of*

# THE ORDER OF THE POISON OAK

<u>The Poison Oak Vow</u>

I vow to always be on the lookout for other members of the Order of the Poison Oak, to help them whenever possible, but to never reveal except to another member or potential member the true meaning of the Order.

# Also by Brent Hartinger . . .

Hc 0-06-001221-8
Pb 0-06-001223-4

### Geography Club

A groundbreaking first novel about gay and lesbian teens in high school.

### The Last Chance Texaco

An explosive story of troubled teens in foster care.

Hc 0-06-050912-0
Pb 0-06-050914-7

Hc 0-06-056727-9

### Grand & Humble

A spooky novel with a mind-blowing surprise ending.

HarperTempest
An Imprint of HarperCollinsPublishers

www.brenthartinger.com